"Say yes, Blue," Walker said with a groan against her thick, flaxen hair.

The raw need in his voice shot through her with heart-stopping intensity. She felt the warmth of his breath on her neck, sensitizing her skin and making her yearn for more.

"Walker . . . no."

"Yes, Blue." He lifted his head and bracketed her face in his large hands. The calloused pads of his thumbs traced the tender skin below her eyes, his palms cupped her cheeks. "You're staying tonight, staying with me."

She listened to him, breathless as his hand slid down her throat and paused just above the collar of her shirt. The heat of his touch spread across her chest, and farther when he pushed the first button from its hole. "Please don't."

"Please don't what? Please don't want you? Impossible." He slipped the second button open. "Please don't make you want me? That's almost too easy." He freed the third button. "Or are you trying to say please don't leave me, Walker? Don't steal my dreams and push me out into the world alone. Well, I'm sorry, Blue, but I am going to steal your dreams, and your kisses, and if I get lucky, real lucky, I'm going to steal your heart the way you've stolen mine. . . ."

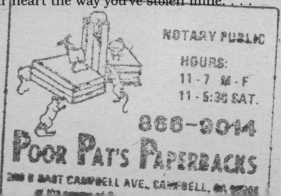

WHAT ARE *LOVESWEPT* ROMANCES?

They are stories of true romance and touching emotion. We believe those two very important ingredients are constants in our highly sensual and very believable stories in the *LOVESWEPT* line. Our goal is to give you, the reader, stories of consistently high quality that may sometimes make you laugh, sometimes make you cry, but are always fresh and creative and contain many delightful surprises within their pages.

Most romance fans read an enormous number of books. Those they truly love, they keep. Others may be traded with friends and soon forgotten. We hope that each *LOVESWEPT* romance will be a treasure—a "keeper." We will always try to publish

LOVE STORIES YOU'LL NEVER FORGET
BY AUTHORS YOU'LL ALWAYS REMEMBER

The Editors

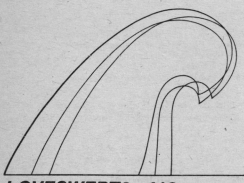

LOVESWEPT® • 413

Glenna McReynolds
Blue Dalton

 BANTAM BOOKS
NEW YORK • TORONTO • LONDON • SYDNEY • AUCKLAND

To Stan, my own man of the mountains—
for giving his love and accepting mine.

BLUE DALTON

A Bantam Book / July 1990

*If you would be interested in receiving protective vinyl
covers for your Loveswept books, please write to this address
for information:*

*Loveswept
Bantam Books
P.O. Box 985
Hicksville, NY 11802*

ISBN 0-553-44043-8

Published simultaneously in the United States and Canada

PRINTED IN THE UNITED STATES OF AMERICA

OPM   0 9 8 7 6 5 4 3 2 1

Prologue

Blue Dalton gritted her teeth and tightened the gauze strip around her hand, stopping the stream of blood that was seeping from the knife cut across her palm. Blood stained the rolled cuff of her blue flannel shirt and dirtied the thigh of her jeans. A red streak ran down the dark skin of her arm and dripped off the curve of her elbow, splashing silently on the toe of her hiking boot. The rough wood floor was smeared with more blood, but it wasn't hers.

Murder. The word forced its way into her mind, past the confusion and fear and horror. Unconsciously she shook her head, replacing the legal terminology with the sane appellation of self-defense. A short swath of hair fell across her face and blurred her vision with a blond veil. She pushed at it with her upper arm and kept wrapping and tying. The unruly strands fell back over her face.

Her softly muttered sound of disgust was cut

short by the sob lodged in her throat. Who was she trying to fool? Certainly not herself, and she damn well doubted she'd fool anybody else.

She held one end of the gauze with her teeth while she used her other hand to tie it off. Unbidden, her gaze flickered over to the man who lay angled off the mattress that was pushed against the wall. Blood soaked the blue-and-white-striped ticking, pooling in the creases of the dirty material.

She'd given him a chance. She'd given him two. But he'd thought his knife hand was faster than her finger on her rifle. He'd been wrong. *Dead wrong . . .*

"No," she whispered, the word catching on a pained gasp of disbelief. "No . . . no . . . no."

The evidence said otherwise, the violence, the blood, the mother lode of adrenaline racing through her veins. One instant of pure animal panic had turned her into a murderer. The knife had arced silently through the air, and in response she'd squeezed the slim band of metal. Pain had sliced into her palm as the gun had jerked and exploded, then there had been nothing but echoes.

There was so much blood. He'd collapsed face down on the bed, and she didn't have the stomach to touch him, let alone roll him over to see what she'd hit. His dark, beard-stubbled face loomed in her memory, along with his bad teeth and the smell of him. He hadn't been the first man to come after her—he wouldn't be the last—but he'd been the first man she'd ever shot.

Shot and killed. An awful feeling washed through her and brought bile up in her throat—a terrible feeling she couldn't even begin to name. With a shaky hand she smeared a tear across her cheek and strode over to the table, her bootsteps sounding loud and hollow in the old mountain cabin.

With mindless skill she packed her gear into her backpack, tying her slicker over the top and her sleeping bag on the bottom of the frame. She hooked her water bottle to the shoulder strap for easy access; once she started walking, she wouldn't be stopping for a long time.

Two other items remained on the table: her hat and a packet, rolled and tied in three places, with the initials L. L. burned into the leather. She lifted the packet and curled her fingers around the soft hide, her mouth trembling at the corners. A man had died for want of the prize and for wanting her—for wanting to hurt her.

She would have given him the packet and tracked him down later—nobody stole from Blue Dalton and got away with it—but she'd have shot herself before physically submitting to him. Luck had decided otherwise, though, and she'd shot him instead.

The first light of dawn skimmed across the white and green land and spilled into the valley, bringing streams of pale sunshine through the cabin window. Blue lifted tear-filled eyes for a moment, then quickened her preparations, sliding a knife sheath on her belt and fighting the panic making her hands shake. She cinched the leather strap tight before fastening the buckle.

A rustling sound snapped her gaze to the open front door, and instantly she had her hand on the haft of the knife. A heartbeat later the breath soughed from her lips as the source of the noise came into view.

"Thank God." She fell to her knees and extended

her hand to the white dog panting on the porch. A steak of blood marred his coat. "Come here, Trapper. Come on, boy." The dog limped forward, and Blue folded him into her arms, hugging him and cooing to him, needing the security he represented. "I thought he had you for sure. Are you okay? Hmm? We've got a rough day ahead of us, Trap." Her fingers tunneled through the soft white coat, and she rested her cheek on his neck. "Don't worry. We're going to make it," she vowed.

She rose, then bent at the knees to pull the pack onto her back. A wince of pain crossed her face as she eased her arms through the shoulder straps. Her body was weak from the fight, from the tension sapping her strength and willpower. The fifty-pound load shifted into position, and with effort she straightened her legs and buckled the hip strap. She bit down on her lower lip. She couldn't stop now. She had to get farther up into the hills. After all these years it was time to return to the North Star ranch and find her future.

Forcing herself not to look back at the man, she shoved her hand through her hair, pushing if off her face, and settled the faded and sweat-stained Stetson low on her head. On her way out the door she slipped her hand through the strap on her rifle, swinging it up and over her shoulder.

"Homicide?"

"Not yet. He was still breathing when the ambulance left. The medic was more worried about the liquor on his breath than the bullet in his shoulder."

"How in the hell did they get an ambulance up here?"

"Carefully."

Walker Evans listened to the exchange and calmly chewed on a long blade of meadow grass. A dozen deputies, rangers, and even some of the state's finest were milling around the cabin, looking for a clue to what Walker already knew and what they'd be hard-pressed to find in the dark—the direction Blue Dalton and her dog had taken off in. Jeff Bowles, the head forest ranger on the scene, had given him the first chance at the cabin, and he'd tracked her a hundred yards into the trees before coming back to the dirt road to wait with the rest of them. That was okay with him. He had all the patience he needed, unless they started messing up her trail after the hundred-yard mark.

So far, none of them had gotten even close. A slight smile curved a corner of his mouth. Bowles wasn't stupid. When you need more rangers, you call your rangers, and when you have to, you call in the state patrol and the county sheriff. But when you need somebody to track a crazy woman through country she knows like the back of her hand, you call a tracker who knows the same country. Yes, Walker was content to wait. He was between seasons and on county time, and he knew he'd catch her.

Blue Dalton, the name went through his mind, bringing another, wryer smile to his face. What he knew about the woman wasn't much, but it was enough. She was her father's daughter, and old Abel must have told her everything. Things were bound to get real interesting in these mountains when word got out she was back. Before things got too interesting, though, he meant to have the situation firmly in hand. He'd waited too long to let someone else jump his claim. He didn't care if everyone else called it Dalton's Treasure. The real name for the riches was Lacey's Lode, and it belonged to him.

"What do you make of this stuff?" The sheriff asked Bowles, tapping his knuckles on the plastic window of Blue Dalton's Jeep, just inches away from where Walker rested against the door.

"Scuba diving gear," Bowles answered, not needing to look inside.

"For what?"

Bowles glanced at Walker. "We think she went diving in the lake. Most of the air is out of the tanks, and the wet suit is still wet." He paused and squinted up into the night sky, peering through the vapor clouds of his breath. "The darn thing is probably frozen by now."

"Lake Agnes?" The sheriff's voice rose with skepticism. "It's illegal to dive in these high lakes."

"So's shooting people," Walker drawled, adding his two bits of enlightenment.

The sheriff shot him a sideways glance, anger apparent in every hard line of his face. "What's the pretty boy doing here?" he snapped at Bowles, staring at Walker as if he wished he'd disappear.

"He's our tracker."

"What's wrong with our regular people?" The sheriff didn't bother to hide his dislike of Walker, and Walker, immune to the sheriff's opinions, let the dislike and the insult slide. But he did wonder if the lawman hated him because his wife had a roving eye, or because Walker had been turning her down since he'd been sixteen and the lady had been twenty-one.

Bowles answered, "Well, sir. Our regular people are good enough to track lost campers who want to be found, but we're dealing with Blue Dalton, and I'd bet a dollar to a dime she doesn't want anybody finding her."

The sheriff accepted the explanation by ignoring it, but Walker distinctly heard him mutter something about sending one no-account after another. Louder, the sheriff said, "What does she want to go diving into Agnes for anyway? There's nothing in there but fish."

"Who knows?" Bowles shrugged and cast a warning look at Walker, which Walker acknowledged with a subtle lowering of his gaze. They both had a damn good idea of what Blue Dalton had gone looking for, but neither saw any reason to bog down the sheriff's investigation with a bunch of hearsay, and ancient hearsay at that. Old man Dalton's dying words had been floating around these mountains long enough for anybody who cared to hear them, though few took them as seriously as Walker. Few had the right.

"What about the Jeep? Why'd she leave it?" the sheriff asked.

Another grin flashed across Walker's face, but he kept his mouth shut. Bowles cleared his throat. "The tires are slashed."

The sheriff looked down and stepped back to check the other side of the Jeep, but he didn't say a word.

"I think we've got a clear case of self-defense," Bowles said. "The man thought he'd found a lone woman up here in the wilderness and decided to get mean. He slashed her tires, beat her dog, then tried to attack her in the cabin."

"Then why did she light out?" the sheriff asked.

"Maybe she got scared," Bowles offered.

Walker coughed into his hand and turned his back.

"Something like that would scare any woman," Bowles insisted, looking at the sheriff but speaking for Walker's benefit.

"Got her so scared she packed up and headed off into nowhere instead of down the road for help? I'm not buying it," the sheriff said.

Neither was Walker. He'd been weaned on tales, true and otherwise, about the Dalton clan, and running scared wasn't exactly their modus operandi. They'd mostly kept to themselves up on their ranch in the Rawahs, but if trouble came looking, they faced it. And trouble, it seemed, did have a tendency to go looking for Daltons.

Well, trouble had a partner now. Walker Evans was looking for a Dalton . . . Blue Dalton.

One

Blue was numb, physically and emotionally. Her feet and legs burned with a deep ache. Her palm pounded with pain. The straps of her pack had worn grooves into her shoulders. She stared at the carpet of pine needles below her boots, stealing time, precious time, to catch her breath.

Her tears had dried yesterday in salty tracks down her cheeks. Today she had sweat in their place. She lifted her good hand to wipe the moisture off her face, stopping in mid-motion as a harsh cry jerked her gaze to the sky and sent her heart pounding. She held herself perfectly still as she looked into the limitless expanse of blue. A hawk circled into view, and she let out her hard-won breath. She'd seen no one, had heard little but whispers of sound wafting through the trees, but she knew someone was behind her and closing in. She felt his presence, steady and stalking, as he searched for her.

Damn you! Whoever you are. Leave me alone!

Her throat closed around the unspoken words, and she kicked at the pine needles in frustration. Immediately realizing the stupidity of her action, she bent down and brushed away the scuff mark and was left with the monumental task of raising herself and her pack back up. She groaned and swore under her breath, her muscles straining, her hand on her thigh barely helping her.

"Damn you," she muttered aloud at the man she didn't know, for she had no doubts the tracker was a man. Intuition and common sense told her so. They would have sent a man after her, a damn canny man if they were serious about catching her, and she had no doubts they were serious, or at least that he was. She'd used every trick she knew, and he was still back there, relentless, unwavering, beating her at her own game.

An eerie fluttering of nerves brought her head around. She scanned the mountainous terrain behind her, searching for a movement or a shadow out of place. But there was only Trapper, his head hanging low, his labored panting intensifying her guilt. She'd been pushing too hard. They needed rest, sleep, and not the catnaps they'd been stealing.

From out of the sky thunder rumbled, rolling over the craggy peaks and bringing a blanket of dark clouds across the valley. Blue covered her eyes with her hand and slowly rubbed her temples. This was it, then. They had to stop and make camp. If they got wet at this altitude, they'd both be dead by morning.

The cloud shadow swept over her, and rain sheeted down the mountainside in quick pursuit, soaking her in seconds. Sighing in weariness, she dropped her hand to her waist and looked around for a protected place. The outcropping of granite she spotted up ahead was more than she'd expected or hoped for. "Come on, boy." She snapped her fingers to get Trapper's attention. "We're calling it a day."

The rain may stop her against every instinct she had, but, by God, it was going to stop *him* too.

Walker was moving forward on pure intuition. Rain slashed through the trees, turning to sleet and back again with every temperature fluctuation and every altitude change. He jostled the pack on his back, rearranging the weight for a moment's respite, and pulled his hat lower on his forehead. Water streamed off the brim, obscuring his view after a few yards.

He was traveling alone now, having convinced Bowles he could move faster without five other men crashing around behind him. And that's the way he liked it, especially this time. Blue Dalton hadn't gone down into the depths of a glacial lake on a whim. The lake was dark, isolated in a high bowl of the Never Summer Range, and colder than the January wind screaming through North Park. It was a wonder she hadn't died in the water.

But if there was one thing he was beginning to realize about Blue Dalton, it was that she was damn hard to kill, or even get close to. A strange part of him was actually anticipating getting a look at her, this amazon of the mountains. A not so strange part of him was predictably excited about getting a look at what she'd found at the bottom of the lake—for he had no doubts she'd found something. Why else had the old coot been hot on her trail, if not to steal Abel Dalton's stolen-treasure hoard? He'd had two days to worry all the pieces into place, and they all added up to the fortune he and half the male population of North Park had spent years looking for. Except all the others were looking for the wrong thing, fooled by Dalton's dying gasp of finding the sky beneath the earth. They were looking for the gold of the sun when they should have been looking for the silver moon and pieces of the summer sky.

A slow smile spread across his face despite the cold sinking through his jacket and shirt and into his bones. Walker shifted his backpack again and struck out into the woods. He'd find her all right, her and his father's treasure.

Close to dark he lowered his expectations to finding a place to camp for the night. Under other circumstances he'd have headed home. Blue Dalton had commenced trespassing on his property late in the afternoon, leading him to within two miles of his cabin.

He should have caught up with her by now, he thought with no small measure of disgust. He'd never live it down if he'd lost her trail.

Wiping his hand across his mouth, he peered into the dripping forest ahead of him, then glanced over his shoulder. If he had lost her trail, he'd done it within the last mile. Her dog had left scat sign, and Blue had missed covering it up—her first mistake. She must be about ready to drop, he thought.

And if you were going to drop, where would you do it? He slowly turned on his heels, scanning the landscape. Below him about twenty yards away a wet slope of granite pushed out of the mountainside, beckoning to him and any other rain-soaked soul.

Without moving another step he knew he'd found her. He pulled his rifle out of his pack and over his shoulder. She was armed and had her dog. He wasn't taking any chances, but neither was he going to sit back and follow her home. There was no dream of glory in the decision, just the cold facts. If she was as worn down as he figured, and if she was hurt, she was in no shape to be out in the elements, and neither was he. Spring rains had a tendency to turn into spring snows in the Rockies.

At ten yards he slipped out of his pack, knowing the dripping trees covered the slight sound. Still, he approached the rock carefully. He didn't want to get shot, and he didn't want to have to shoot her. She'd come too far to lose her life to him.

Sodden pine needles cushioned his silent steps, one after the other. A glimpse of her jury-rigged lean-to brought satisfaction but no smile to his face. One edge of her gray slicker had come loose from its mooring and was flapping in the breeze. A small hand and a white paw were pushed out of the bottom of the lean-to; both were covered with mud and soaking wet.

Walker stopped, holding himself still, and stared at the hand. An uneasy sensation skittered across his nerve endings. The hand was too small, about half the size of his, and that couldn't be right. That couldn't be Blue Dalton's hand.

Keeping to the high side of the slope, he moved around the rock, his finger on the trigger of his rifle. As the underside of the boulder came into view, he moved farther back.

"Stop where you stand," a low voice hissed out of the shadows, followed by a menacingly soft growl. Walker froze.

The wrong end of a rifle swung into view, the stock cradled next to her waist, her bandaged hand nested around the trigger with one finger precisely in place. Neither she nor the dog had moved from their prone positions on the ground, but they were both looking dead center at him, two pairs of dark-brown eyes, one set holding his steady gaze, the other pair angled more toward his throat. Walker swallowed, a reflexive action he couldn't stop but the only one he allowed.

"Drop the rifle," she ordered.

"No." He slowly moved his head from side to side.

"The dog will get you if I don't," she warned, and Walker noted the barest tremble in her voice. He shot a quick glance at the dog. The animal looked mean, real mean, but he also looked half dead. Walker remembered the club they'd found outside the cabin, the one matted with bloody white hair. He also remembered the gash on the shot man's left leg. Walker had tangled with a dog once. He didn't care to repeat the experience.

"I—I'm not here to hurt you," he said, forcing a halting measure of fear into his voice.

"Prove it. Drop the gun."

"I can't."

"Can't?"

"Too scared." It was a small lie, but one he hoped would increase her confidence enough to make her careless.

Her unladylike reply told him he hadn't fooled her for a second. He decided on another plan and slowly swung the aim of his rifle from her chest to the dog's.

"The dog goes first, Blue," he said softly, committing himself.

He never knew what tipped him off, but when she fired, he was already halfway toward the ground. The recoil of her rifle did the rest, throwing her shot off the mark.

Scrambling and swearing, he lunged for the lean-to, grabbing her leg and jerking her out into the open before the dog could sink his teeth into his arm. He swung her in front of him for protection and ripped the rifle out of her hand.

"Are you crazy?" he yelled, his heart beating fast and furiously in his chest. "Call your dog off!"

The dog stood a foot away, too damn close for Walker's peace of mind. He could smell the animal's breath, see the mile of teeth circling its jaws, hear the snap and growl coming from deep in its throat. Then he noticed the dog was only using three legs. The fourth paw was held off the ground and a pinkish smear of blood covered the leg from top to bottom.

"Call off your dog!" he shouted again, but no one heard him. He glanced down at the woman in his arms and swore under his breath. She'd passed out cold. He was holding her so tightly, he hadn't even noticed her lack of resistance. Maybe he'd squeezed the breath out of her, or maybe she was playing possum.

He lightened his grip and tried not to think about the dog standing there, waiting for an opportunity to tear his throat out.

"Dammit!" She wasn't playing possum. Her head lolled forward. Her legs were buckled beneath her, skinny little legs. Her arms hung limply at her sides, skinny little arms. She was a bag of bones. He doubted if she weighed a hundred pounds, and she was already soaking wet. Water streamed down the back of her neck and soaked the flannel of her shirt, unhindered by any feminine length of hair. She'd cut it short. A wide swath of the dirty-blond strands hung over her ear and hid her face. "Dammit!" he repeated.

He scooted back, and the dog growled, a low rumbling, never-ending sound.

"I'm not going to hurt her, boy." Walker tried his most soothing tone. "Trust me. I'm not going to hurt her."

The growling increased in volume. The dog was no fool. Walker swore silently. If he'd been the dog, he wouldn't have believed him either.

"Okay, boy. This is what we're going to do. I'm going to take Blue with me. Blue, see?" He gave Blue a little shake. She moaned, and the dog stopped growling and pricked up his ears. "That's right, boy. Blue is going with me." He pushed back another foot. The dog followed with a hopping limp. "Now you can do whatever you want . . . except try and stop me. You can come with us, or you can stay here and guard the camp. Doesn't matter to me either way."

When he had five feet between them, Walker slowly rose to his feet, dragging Blue with him with his arm around her waist. She slumped down until his arm was under both of hers. The dog followed another step. That's what Walker liked about German shepherds: They were smart.

Moving carefully and slowly, Walker swung her over his shoulder and bent down to pick up the two rifles. He eyed her pack wistfully, but knew he didn't have a choice. He'd have to shoot the dog to get to it, and he'd have to leave Blue on the mountain in order to carry it home. Nope, he didn't have a choice.

"We're going now, boy," he said to the dog. "You're welcome to come, like I said. But I've got to get Blue home." He walked backward two more steps and bent down and snagged his hat. He released the rifles for a moment to jam the hat on his head, then he picked the guns up again. He looked at the backpack one more time, cussed softly, and straightened up.

"Okay, this is it. We're leaving, not going far, about two miles south, that's all," he said, hefting Blue to a more comfortable position. He sidestepped around the dog, not quite trusting the animal enough to turn his back on him.

But after a couple of minutes of edging sideways through the trees and almost tripping twice, he had to take a chance. He didn't make a production number out of it. He just turned his back and took a step, then another, and another.

Daylight deserted him a mile from home. The dog never did.

Two

Walker put another log on the fire and collapsed back into his chair, splaying his legs in utter exhaustion. Every muscle and bone in his body ached. His neck might never be right again. Blue Dalton's limp body had gotten heavier and heavier with every quarter mile. By the time he'd dragged himself up his porch steps, she'd weighed a ton.

But she sure didn't look like much stretched out on his couch, dampening the faded plaid with her wet, slender form. He'd taken her boots off, and three layers of socks later realized why he'd thought he was tracking a much larger woman. How she'd ever kept ahead of him for two days wearing boots a size too big was beyond him. He didn't want to think how he'd feel about himself when he went back in the morning to get their packs, for he already knew whose was the heaviest —hers, laden with the treasure.

How in the hell had she kept ahead of him? The thought crossed his mind for the hundredth time as he stared at her. He shook his head and reached for his coffee. The telephone was next to the cup, but he ignored it the same way he'd been ignoring it for the last hour. The fire lit into some sap and flared up with a crackle and a pop. The dog jerked awake.

"Go back to sleep, boy," Walker said. "It's just the fire."

The dog looked over at him, then settled back down on the rug in the far corner of the cabin. Walker listened to his soft groans and hoped they didn't mean anything. The dog needed doctoring— Blue did too—but he was too cautious to touch the one and too sensible to touch the other. The drying blood-stained rag wrapped around Blue's hand would have to remain until she woke up, a moment he was awaiting with both anticipation and a strange sense of unease. He didn't know what to make of her. From the tips of her toes to the crop of golden hair, she wasn't what he'd expected to find.

He lifted the mug to his mouth, sipped slowly, and tried not to stare at her so hard—a fruitless endeavor. He couldn't take his eyes off her. She didn't look like an amazon, the type of woman who could shoot a man, or a treasure hunter. She looked like a skinny kid, kind of a pretty, skinny kid. And without her rifle pointed at him she looked incredibly vulnerable.

His gaze roamed from her small, dirty feet, up the length of her legs to where her jeans were bunched around her waist with a big belt, to the gentle rise and fall of her chest. Her thick blond hair, parted far to one side, had fallen back from her face, revealing a small nose and feathery wings of black lashes resting on darkly tanned cheeks. What held his gaze, though, was her mouth and the diminutive beauty mark above her upper lip. Her mouth did something to him he didn't want to admit. Her lower lip was full, teasing even in repose, tempting his imagination to wander in ridiculous, dangerous directions.

He snorted in self-recrimination, leaned forward, and flipped the blanket over her feet. *She's Blue Dalton,* he silently reminded himself, adding the warning of, *Don't forget it.*

She stirred restlessly at his slight touch, murmuring as she kicked the blanket off. Heaving a deep sigh, he settled back into his chair. What was he going to do with her now that he'd finally caught her, he wondered. He didn't really need her. He had the backpack, or at least he knew where it was.

Call Bowles and have him take her off your hands. She's his problem. The voice of reason spoke calmly in his mind.

Right, he thought.

Then why does she feel like your problem? The voice of reason stumbled into an undeniable truth. She did feel like his problem, a personal problem, and it bothered him that he couldn't figure out why.

He crossed his legs at the ankles and slid farther down into his overstuffed chair. Lord, he was tired—his glance strayed up to her face—and she was exhausted, hurt . . . *and pretty, very pretty.* The unwelcome admission furrowed his brow, but didn't slow his imagination. There wasn't a single part of her he didn't think would fit in the palm of his hand: not the delicate curve of her cheek, not the breadth of her shoulder, not the fullness of the small breasts apparent under her shirt.

"Call Bowles," he muttered, sitting back up, determined to finish the job they were paying him plenty to do. He picked up the phone, dialed the number, and put the receiver next to his ear. The phone rang once, twice.

Blue mumbled in her sleep, finishing with a short gasp as she grabbed her waist.

"Hello?" Bowles answered.

Walker dropped the receiver back in its cradle and in two strides was kneeling by the couch. His gaze raced down her body and back up, looking for anything he might have missed, but he still didn't touch her. After the direction his mind had chosen to wander in, he didn't trust himself to touch her, and that bothered him in a dozen other ways he didn't want to explore.

"Abel," she whispered, her mouth parting softly. Her hand tightened on her waist, bunching cloth and something else in her fingers. Walker followed the movement. His eyes narrowed and a curious smile curved a corner of his mouth.

"Ah, Blue," he murmured, the smile broadening into a full-fledged grin.

With more caution than sense he lowered his hand next to hers and gently pulled her shirt out of her jeans, inch by inch, his anticipation building. All the time he'd been worrying about leaving her pack behind, she'd had the goods right on her. Damn! He should have checked her out from top to—

The thought fell apart when her undershirt came out with the blue flannel, exposing a triangle of silky skin above her belt. Walker stopped pulling, the smile slowly fading from his face. Firelight danced through the shadows created by the raised cotton cloth, adding mystery to the unexpected view of Blue Dalton. She stretched; the overlarge jeans slipped lower on her hips, revealing a satiny curve of waist, and Walker let out a slow, measured breath.

This is crazy, he told himself even as he felt the subtle change in his body, a tightening he had no business feeling. He'd seen bare skin before, more than he cared to remember most of the time, and it was just her stomach, for crying out loud . . . *just an enticing glimpse of the no-man's-land between forbidden territories.* The fanciful thought caused his gaze to roam up to her breasts and down again to the softly worn jeans covering her hips, her thighs, her calves.

Walker shook off the moment of sexual awareness. However fascinating the stuff below her undershirt, there was something equally fascinating between the white cotton and the blue flannel.

An edge of leather came into view, a rolled packet grasped by her hand through her shirt. He pondered the dilemma for a moment, glancing up at her face. She was asleep all right. He eased his fingers under her shirt and slipped the packet away from her. His smile broadened into a grin when the packet came free into his hands. It was small, too small to hold everything he had dreamed about, but it was a start.

Excited, he turned on the balls of his feet and sat down with his back resting against the couch. He held the packet for a long moment, relishing the final success, the final justice. He'd been pretty bereft of successes this year, and justice always seemed to be in the eye of the beholder. This time they'd both fallen into his hand. The initials burned into the leather proved his father's story of betrayal. L. L., for Lacey's Lode. There had been only one Lacey of renown in North Park, Lacey Evans, she of the gentle touch who'd dried every tear he'd ever shed except the last ones he'd cried for losing her. The pain had gone years before, but the memories and the riches two men had promised her remained.

Slowly, ever so slowly, he unknotted the leather laces, letting each one slide into his lap as it came undone. He straightened his legs to unroll the packet down his thighs—and that's how she caught him, fingers poised above the flaps covering the treasure, mesmerized by what he had yet to see.

Walker felt the cool, sharp edge slide down his neck, touching but not cutting, not yet. He saw the knife blade glint with yellow light from the fire.

"Tie it back up." Her voice was raspy and weak. The knife pressed against his skin was neither.

"I should have frisked you," he said calmly, realizing the limits of her strength even if she didn't. He just hoped she had enough sense to keep the knife from slipping accidentally.

"Seems you already did all the frisking I'm gonna allow." The blade slid farther down his neck and pointed at the packet spread across his legs. "Tie it up and hand it over."

Walker mulled over his options for about half a minute, long enough to flex the fingers of his right hand, readying them. Then he made his move, smoothly and quickly, encircling her knife hand and jerking her off the couch and across his lap.

She landed with a surprised gasp of pain, her eyelids fluttering closed. She bit down on her lower lip, that tempting lower lip, making him regret the force he'd used.

Blue felt the contrition she'd hoped for lighten his grip, and she took immediate advantage of his mistake. With a twist of her wrist she tossed the knife into her bandaged hand and had the blade back at his throat. A very masculine, very bronze throat, she realized, her gaze flicking upward to a beard-stubbled square jaw. She dared look no further, not with her knife pressing into his skin. If the tracker was dumb enough to move, or even breathe too hard, the razor-edged blade would slice through him like it would through butter on a hot day. She'd been careful with him up to now, but she refused to take responsibility for his next action.

Smart man, she thought a second later. The tracker had decided to stop breathing altogether. The artery in his neck pulsed regardless, but Blue had deliberately not touched him there.

"Mister, I'm tired of fooling with you," she said, holding him at bay and slowly easing herself off his lap. She had to get out of there, away from him and back up into the mountains to safety before the law came down on her.

"The feeling is mutual," Walker muttered, raising both hands shoulder high and letting her go, but only as far as suited him. When she was halfway to her feet, he lashed out with his leg and tumbled her onto her back. Before she could move, he was on top of her, crushing her to the floor and holding both of her wrists with his hands. Guilt assailed him again. She was so small beneath him. But not helpless, he grimly reminded himself as he struggled to restrain her.

Blue tossed her head and twisted her body, cursing him to hell and back. The breath whooshed out of her lungs as he shifted his weight. She gasped and squeezed her eyes shut against the increased pressure. Lights danced behind her closed lids. *Please, God, don't let me faint,* she prayed, even as she swore her vengeance.

Tight jawed, Walker let her wear herself down, listening to her scorching tirade of cussing and wondering when she'd run out of steam. He lifted her arms above her head and gripped both wrists in his right hand. He disarmed her with his left, noting the incredible delicacy of her bones with a confused lift of his brow. His one hand easily encompassed both of hers, just as he'd thought. What kind of woman was she, he wondered, to be so small yet so damn strong?

"Quiet down or you'll wake the dog," he told her, low on patience with her highly specialized vocabulary and the squirming body reminding him of what he'd been trying to forget.

"Trap," she gasped the name, turning her head toward the animal lying motionless near the fire. Reflected flames drew his gaze to the fragile curve of her jaw and the delicate protrusion of her collarbone beneath her shirt. His mental wandering was short-lived. Dark, almost black, eyes flashed back to him. Her sweet mouth twisted into a snarl. "What did you do to him? If you hurt him, *I'll kill you. I swear I will."* She jerked her arms, and he tightened his grip.

"I haven't touched him"—he paused and swore softly when she tried to knee him in the groin. He sat heavier on her, holding her still—"but I'm sure that won't keep you from coming up with a reason to cut me if you get the chance."

"You're hurting me," she said, moaning, fluttering her eyes closed with all the melodrama of a two-bit actress.

Walker didn't doubt it, but he wasn't about to fall into the same trap twice. Of course he couldn't sit on her all night either. His glance fell to her belt, and not caring what she thought, he reached down and undid the buckle. "Lift your hips."

Her eyes flew open, startled and wary. Her skin paled beneath her tan, making her eyes seem darker than the night. "I'll kill you, you son of a motherless polecat. You low-down, worse than a—"

"Hush, Blue. I'm not going to rape you. But I'm not going to let you run around here trying to do me in at every opportunity either." He unthreaded the belt from one side of her jeans. "Lift up," he ordered. When she didn't budge, he wrapped his hand around the waist of her jeans and roughly rolled her onto her side. Then he finished pulling the belt free.

Silently seething, Blue felt the leather wrap around her wrists, tighter and tighter, until he was satisfied and finished binding her with a knot. If he thought tying her up would subdue her, he was in for a rude awakening, but one she'd deliver on her own terms. He'd won the last two skirmishes; she couldn't afford to lose the third. *Conserve your energy,* she told herself. *Breathe slowly.*

Walker eased off of her, unbuckling his own belt one-handed and watching her for signs of a fight. He noted the narrowing of her eyes and knew what she was thinking. "You don't need to look at me like that. I already told you I'm not interested. There are plenty of women around willing to give it away free without me having to fight you." He didn't know what else to say to reassure her, but he tried lying. "You're not exactly the type who drives a man crazy with lust."

She knew that without his telling her, and she hated him just a little bit more, and a little bit more when he trussed her ankles with his belt. With one large hand he pushed her legs to the floor. She never had a chance to kick him.

"You bastard," she hissed as he cinched the belt tighter.

"You'll get no argument on that point," he said, rising from the floor and hauling her with him. He lifted her as if she weighed nothing, and for the first time Blue became aware of him as a man and not solely as her enemy. He was big, well over six feet. Mile-wide shoulders and a broad chest dwarfed her as the tracker swung her up into his arms and brought her eye-level with a face that made her heart stop for a single beat. Her reaction alarmed her even more than his looks and the close way he held her. She dug a hasty retreat into anger.

"Put me down!"

"When I get where I'm going," he replied.

Blue twisted, and his arms tightened like a vise. Light-brown eyes shot through with flecks of gold and green held her gaze with relentless purpose. He spoke very softly in warning. "Don't keep pushing me, Blue. I haven't decided what to do with you yet."

"Who are you?" she demanded, unsure of what he meant and unnerved by the deep huskiness of his voice. Big men usually had voices to match, but this giant seemed to be trying to fool her with a gentleness she didn't feel in the belts tied around her limbs.

"Walker Evans." He strode over to the couch and unceremoniously dumped her in the corner. "Are you hungry?"

She ignored his question with one of her own. "And who is Walker Evans?" she asked with a sneer, trying to avoid staring at his long legs and the muscles revealed by the worn denim of his jeans. But he hadn't backed away from the couch, and the sheer size of him filled her line of vision.

Her question threw Walker for a minute, but it would be just like old man Dalton to never mention the Evans name. He didn't like talking about his failures either. "I'm the man the law hired to track you down," he said, offering her the simplest explanation.

Blue forced her gaze to raise past his thighs, button fly, and empty belt loops. A slow blush crept up her cheeks as she met his eyes once more. "Took you long enough," she said with a trifle less acidity on her tongue than she'd wanted.

"You're good," he agreed with a shrug of his broad shoulders. "But I'm better."

Blue refrained from replying to the obvious. Her "fight-or-flight" systems were shutting down one by one, making her more aware of her surround-

ings and almost painfully aware of the man tower-
ing over her. She could just imagine what kind of
woman it took to drive him crazy with lust; the
poor dumb thing would probably have to be at
least as pretty as he was, and feminine to the
point of pure helplessness. He could have them—
all of them, she added grudgingly—as long as he
left her alone, or better yet, let her go.

Her eyes flicked over him again, her mouth curling in distaste. She didn't even like long hair on
herself, let alone on a man. And his was definitely
on the long side, like tawny silk, sweeping back
from his face and lying on the collar of his faded
aqua shirt. Giving him his due, she found no
fault with the body beneath the shirt. He was big
and strong. Too strong by her reckoning, she
thought, remembering the rock-hard feel of him
when he'd had her on the floor. His thighs had
been like a denim-sheathed vise when he'd strad-
dled her hips. He'd picked her up with arms thickly
corded with muscle as if she weighed nothing.
She didn't have a chance against him on the
brawn side of the battle.

His eyes left a lot to be desired, though. They
were too golden to be brown, and too brown to be
anything else. Amber, she guessed they called the
color, or hazel. She called it unsettling, the same
thing she called the way he was watching her, as
if he could see further than her skin. While she
was mentally on the subject of his looks, she decided his jaw was too wide, his cheekbones were
too sculpted, his mouth too sensual for a real
man, especially the expressive curve of the upper
lip when it hinted at a smile—as it did now.

"Are you hungry?" he repeated his earlier question.

"I can't eat like this." She lifted her bound wrists with a defiant air even as she wondered about the last, unexpected turn of her thoughts. True, he was better looking than most, but Blue had never been one to be swayed by a man's looks, and his manhandling left her no reason to start now—soul-searching eyes, rugged beauty or not.

"You'll figure it out if you're hungry enough." He bent down and picked up her packet.

"That belongs to me," she said through gritted teeth.

"And you belong to me." He faced her with unreadable shadows in his eyes, dark shadows heightened by the wings of his eyebrows and the thickness of his lashes.

"I don't belong to anybody," she retorted, lifting her chin and leveling him with a lethal glare, which he didn't seem to notice.

"Tonight you do, Blue," he said, his voice gravelly rough and silky soft at the same time. "You're mine until I call the cops."

"So call the damn cops."

"Don't tempt me." He rolled the packet over in his large, weathered hand, seeming to forget her existence.

Gold fever. She saw it in his eyes, in the tender touch of his fingers on the leather. She knew what they'd all made of her father's last words, and the thought brought a smug smile to her lips. Walker Evans was no better than all the others who'd tried to steal her inheritance; he didn't even know what he was looking for.

As he hefted the bound leather package the cuff

rode up on his arm, and Blue caught a glint of metal and stone. He had a *ketoh* wrapped around his wrist, the broad bands of silver shining against his bronzed skin. For a long moment she stopped breathing, her gaze fixed on the wide rectangle of silver and the turquoise stone a good three inches in length and two in width. He wore the piece as a bracelet, attached to four connected rolls of silver instead of to leather, but it was Navaho, and it was old, the age attested to by the greenish cast of the stone and the simple workmanship of the *ketoh* itself. The bracelet part was newer, the work of a contemporary artisan. She found her breath again with the observation. Lots of people owned silver-and-turquoise jewelry. The *ketoh* wasn't part of her inheritance.

In truth, she doubted if it could have belonged to many people besides Walker Evans. The piece was large, rough, masculine, and it required a man to match, a man with more than a hint of wildness in him despite the genetically refined planes of his face, a man with the confidence to wear his hair too long and the ability to cut through her defenses with even a casual glance—a man she needed to escape.

She sat quietly, marshaling her strength while he unfolded the soft leather flaps. At the last second he cast her a quick, possibly guilty, glance with his strange amber eyes. Then he opened the packet.

"What in the hell is this?" he asked with a growl, the guilt replaced by a steely edge of anger.

"I don't know what you're talking about." Innocence never had a sweeter mouth or a more demure tone.

"This is what I'm talking about." He held a yellowed sheet of paper in his hand, letting the leather packet drop to the floor. "You didn't risk your life in Lake Agnes for a piece of paper. A blank piece of paper!"

"I didn't risk my life in Agnes, period." Who did he think he was talking to? Some idiot who didn't know how to take care of herself?

"If you believe that, then you're not as smart as I've been giving you credit for being. Dammit," he said, slapping the paper on his thigh.

"Don't!" Blue gasped, her hands automatically reaching out. "Don't do— Stop!" she said again when the paper crinkled in his fist.

Walker's gaze fell to the paper, then lifted to meet her eyes. "Why, Blue?" he asked, tilting his head in question, his voice dangerously soft again. "There's nothing on it."

"It's . . . it's old. That's all; it's old."

The flush in her cheeks, a pale flood of pink under fawn-colored skin, told him she was lying. He looked at the paper and still saw nothing.

But there had to be something.

Lightning flashed nearby, crackling through the night and sending an electric blue-white glow through the south-side window. Walker glanced up reflexively, then back at the paper. There had to be something.

Thunder rumbled in behind the lightning and seemed to roll right up to the cabin's walls, shaking them with the power of sound. Blue shivered and held her breath, watching confusion cross his face and slowly turn to understanding. She swallowed hard. "Whatever you're thinking, you're wrong."

"I don't think so," he muttered, walking over to the fireplace. He held the paper up, and she saw a corner of his mouth lift. He looked over his shoulder at her. A length of tawny hair fell forward, and he pushed it back with his hand. "Crude," he said, the curve of his mouth spreading into a slow, easy grin, "but effective."

Blue felt herself blush at his smile, as she was sure a thousand women had done before her, and her anger increased. He was too damn sure of himself. "You've got nothing without me."

"We'll see." He walked over to a desk on the other side of the fireplace and flattened the paper on the top. Wax writing, he thought with a shake of his head, scribbling a pencil back and forth across the yellowed sheet. Each revealed letter and number increased his excitement—and his confusion. When he got to the bottom of the page, he silently conceded a point in her favor. He had nothing. "What does this mean?" he asked, not raising his gaze from the paper.

"How should I know? I haven't seen it." Damn him, she thought, using his distraction to work the belt off her ankles. Her whole body hurt, every square inch. She had blisters on top of blisters, and after wrestling around on the floor, probably bruises on top of bruises.

She stopped for a second and shook her head, trying to free her mind from exhaustion, then continued working. When her legs were free, she stretched and tugged on the belt around her wrists. It gave, but not enough. Her chin dropped to her chest. She needed more time. She needed a hot meal and the two nights of sleep he'd stolen from her. "Read it to me, and I'll see what I can make of it."

Read it to me, and I'll see what I can make of it? What was she up to now? Walker glanced over his shoulder and found her struggling with her bonds. Lord, he thought with a quiet sigh. The woman just didn't know when to quit.

He watched her in silence for a couple of seconds, more curious than worried about what she'd do when she got free. The guns were in the kitchen, and he had quicker access to them than she did. He'd brought the knife with him to the desk. She'd come up with something, though, something he wouldn't like. He didn't doubt it for a minute.

"They're directions of some sort," he said. She bit down on her lower lip, and he saw her straining, twisting her shoulders for leverage against the belt. "A few of the letters are broken where the wax fell off."

"That's your fault," she muttered. "You shouldn't have crunched it up."

His money was on Blue. Any belt, any knot, would give under that kind of relentless attack. "I think if a person knew where the starting point was, they could figure out the rest of it." She stopped her struggles, and he quickly glanced down at the paper, not wanting her to know he was aware of what she was doing. For some reason he wanted her to think she had a chance. He didn't want to crush her minor victory until he had to.

"What are you talking about?"

So he was right, he thought. "We both know what I'm talking about. Dalton's treasure." He used the common term so there wouldn't be any misunderstanding.

"At least you know who it belongs to," she snapped.

"It belongs to whoever finds it," he countered. "No other claim will stand up in a court of law." And it belonged to him by right of inheritance; he wouldn't accept any other claim. If someone other than Blue had been after it, he'd have stopped them too.

"Better men than you have tried." Her snide tone broke into his thoughts and brought his head around. "And they've all failed. I'm the only person who even has a chance."

"Because you know the starting point?"

"Because I knew my father!" She inadvertently rose to her feet.

Walker held her gaze until she realized what she'd done. Then he spoke to her in that unsettlingly soft voice. "There are no better men than me, Blue, and you're not going to find anything without me, without this." He lifted the paper with the tips of his fingers and let it fall back to the desk.

Blue was so mad, she could spit. He'd provoked her into losing her advantage. "You bastard!"

"We've already discussed my parentage . . . and had moved on to yours. What did your father tell you?" An edge of steel underlay his gentle tone.

Anyone with an ounce of common sense would have backed down right then and there. He was easily twice her size and had shown little hesitation in his dealings with her. He'd caught her, tied her, and uncovered the last of the string of clues she'd been following for five years. No one else had done as well—*and lived to tell about it.*

The chilling thought came out of nowhere and brought her anger up short. She blanched, suddenly remembering everything she'd fought to forget during her desperate escape from Lake Agnes. There had been blood, lots of it. Her glance fell to her bandaged hand, and her breath lodged in her throat. Gasping for air, she sank back onto the couch. She'd killed a man. "Oh, my Lord," she whispered.

Three

Walker watched in growing confusion as the terror of the Rawahs crumpled before his very eyes. Something bad was happening to her. One second she'd been fighting him with those devilish dark sparks in her eyes, and in the next she'd gone limp and lifeless, slipping to the couch in total defeat.

"Blue? What's wrong?" He strode across the room as he spoke, trying to get there in time to catch her if she fell.

The horrible scenes flashed through Blue's mind. She didn't hear the concern in his voice as he called her name. She didn't hear his approach or feel the touch of his hand on her shoulder.

"My God, my God," she said with a moan, burying her head in her hands. For the first time the full impact of what she'd done hit her. She'd run before, consumed only with escaping. Now she had no choice but to face the truth: She'd shot and killed a man. It didn't matter that he'd have

37

done the same to her—after he was finished with her. "I killed him. . . . I killed him." The whispered words caught on the sob welling up in her throat, but Walker heard them and felt a moment's relief. He understood the effects of delayed shock, how it could creep up on a person or drop from nowhere like a ton of bricks.

He knelt and grasped both of her arms with his hands, squeezing her tighter than he meant to, but, Lord, she'd given him a scare. He'd never seen anyone go so white.

"No, you didn't," he said, looking up at her and giving her a little shake. "Listen to me, Blue. You didn't kill him," he repeated with more force. But she was too far gone. Her choking sobs filled the cabin, heavy sobs accompanied by her tears. The wet trails ran down her face, matting her lashes and tracing tracks in the dirt smudged across her cheeks. She trembled in his hands, and his heart did something strange. Mentally he tried to pull away from her, and much to his surprise he found he couldn't. He was trapped as surely as he was kneeling there, trapped by her sadness and the unexpected evidence of her remorse streaming down her cheeks.

Walker had seen a lot of female tears, usually on the tail end of a good-bye—his good-bye—and if anyone had asked, he'd have said he was exempt from their particular pull on a man's heart. But a crying Blue Dalton, damn her hide, made him feel helpless. There were no easy answers for what he felt, and he wasn't in the mood to think about the more complicated ones.

So he did the only thing he could think of doing, the thing all those other women had wanted and he hadn't given: He wrapped his arms around her, well aware of how foolish he felt. His hands felt awkward; he didn't know what to do with them, a problem he'd never had with a woman before.

Blue slumped against him, hiding her face against his shoulder and crying as if her heart would break. He had no choice but to pull her off the couch and into his lap. Her slender body molded itself to his much larger frame so naturally, so easily, he didn't know quite what to make of it. He'd expected her to feel bony, all knees and elbows, but she didn't. She felt soft and delicate . . . fragile.

How many more times was she going to surprise him, he wondered, his hands sliding around her back and waist. How many more times was he going to let her? His shoulder became wet with her tears, her body shook in his arms, and still he held her, and still he wondered.

The tears flowed from Blue's eyes unheeded in the morass of emotions swamping her. A tenuous blanket of shock had insulated her from her memories for three days. Now the threads had unraveled, leaving her open to the graphic pictures in her mind: the man's leering face, his slack mouth whispering dirty promises of pleasure and pain—his pleasure, her pain. The knife, the subtle change in his eyes before he'd made his move, her rifle shot, everything came back to her in living color and stereophonic sound.

An involuntary shudder coursed through her body. Her fingers gripped the broad shoulder under her hands, and she felt the arms around her flex and draw her closer yet, surrounding her, giving her a strength she couldn't give herself. She was so tired, so very tired, weary to the bone from running.

"Shh, Blue," he whispered in his strangely gentle voice. "You didn't kill him."

"I didn't mean to," she said on a sob. "He was awful . . . awful, but I wasn't going to kill him, I swear. His knife . . . he cut me. I—I pulled the trigger." She ended on a soft wail, shaking her head against the shoulder supporting her.

"You didn't kill him."

"Blood everywhere, all over the floor . . . the walls."

"You didn't kill him."

"I—"

"—didn't kill him." The tracker's voice spoke softly in her ear, close and warm, reinforcing his words with assurance. Backed up by that voice, the words finally sank in but didn't make her feel any better. She was too exhausted ever to feel better. Nothing made sense. Not her tears, not the overwhelming weakness of her mind and body, and certainly not the man holding her.

"I should have," she whispered between the catches in her breath. "He was going to . . . going to—"

"Shh, Blue. It's over now. You're safe." Another lie, he thought even as he spoke. She wasn't safe. Half of Jackson County was looking for her, and who knew how many more men like the one at the cabin were looking for her—men like himself, looking for the key to Dalton's Treasure.

Walker had stopped entertaining any illusions about himself a long time ago. In truth, he didn't have much argument with the sheriff's summation of "no-account." By most standards he was.

He'd rather the world saw him that way than as what he really was, a man fighting and sometimes losing a long battle to hold on to what was his. What Jack Evans hadn't drunk away in the last twenty years of his life he'd left to his only son: the shadowy remains of a once-great ranch, more mortgage than land, and no cattle left to run on the latter.

But to be put in the same category with a man who had beaten a dog and tried to rape a woman—well, that didn't set well. It didn't set well at all.

Of its own accord his body stiffened at the meaning of his thoughts, transmitting his unease to the woman in his lap. Her sobs stopped suddenly, her muscles tensing beneath his hands, and she raised her tear-streaked face to look at him. An arc of blond hair tangled over her brow, mussed against his shoulder by her crying. Wetness dampened her cheeks and pooled in the corners of her mouth, that sweetly curved mouth mere inches from his own. Luminous brown eyes stared into his very soul, heartbeat after slow, heavy heartbeat, warming him in all the wrong places in all the right ways.

She swallowed softly and lifted her bound hands to wipe away a tear, without ever releasing him from her dark and vulnerable gaze, and Walker thought, *Dear Lord, I'm going to kiss Blue Dalton.*

The thought barely formed before the action followed. His hands didn't have any trouble sliding up to cup her face. They didn't hesitate to pull her closer, his thumbs brushing across the satiny skin of her cheeks. He paused for a second, his gaze meeting hers, telegraphing his intent and giving her a chance to escape, a chance she didn't take. Then his eyes drifted closed and his mouth opened over hers.

She tasted warm and sweet, salty from her tears, and infinitely better than any other woman he'd ever kissed. Her lips parted on a soft gasp, and he slipped his tongue inside—and then he forgot she was Blue Dalton. All the honeyed sweetness of her chased the name from his mind. His tongue delved deeper, stroking hers with gentle, consuming thrusts. He opened his mouth wider, wanting more, asking her to do the same. When she did, the warmth turned to heat. And when her tongue caressed his, the heat turned into a slow, hot flame.

Blue slipped mindlessly from confusion into sensation, her only attempt at refusal a weak and insignificant gasp, which he'd turned into a melting assault on her mouth. His tongue filled her, and the most incredible feeling spread throughout her entire body, shimmery and potent. She touched him in turn, and the feelings doubled over on themselves, welling up in a wave of desire.

Walker groaned his pleasure, and his hand slid down to her waist and back up under her T-shirt, but only far enough for him to feel the silkiness of her skin. He wanted to fill his palm with her breast, but he didn't want to scare her off. At least he had that much sense left. He didn't want her to stop what she was doing: those lazy, teasing tracks of her tongue through his mouth. He didn't want her to realize what she was doing to him, not when she felt this good . . . not when she seared him with each hesitant touch and built a licking fire in his loins . . . not when she did it so effortlessly, so quickly. What he wanted was more of her, closer, and closer still, until she put out the fire.

Blue was lost and losing more ground with each new angle of his mouth over hers. He kissed her, kept kissing her, and she kept kissing him back. The tracker was stealing her thoughts and giving her feelings, feelings unlike any she'd known before. The heat of his body surrounded her. The wet heat of his mouth invaded her. She never wanted to stop, to stop feeling the caresses of his lips, the gentle sucking of her tongue into his mouth, and the resulting langour he created deep down inside her body.

She lifted her bound hands to his collar, held him to her, and captured his husky groan with her mouth. The sound echoed in her mind, igniting her passion with his, and she found herself moving restlessly against him, wanting him closer in ways she didn't dare admit.

Walker felt the change in her streak through him like a high-voltage current. Her bottom rubbing against him and her ragged sigh totally seduced him, pushing him over the edge. He half caught his breath and pulled her tighter, pressing her against him. His body hardened, and he gave up on restraint. It was too easy, too simple to kiss a woman and feel everything inside himself coalesce into one driving need. He wanted her now, to the point of no return.

But one damnable doubt kept him from taking her. She gave too much. She wasn't teasing him, she wasn't holding anything back, and she wasn't asking for anything more than he wanted to give. So even as his hand slid up to cup her breasts, his other hand tangled through her hair and gently eased her lips away from his.

The intimate touch, the satiny fullness filling his hand, caused his eyes to close on a sigh of pleasure. She fit perfectly, was so soft. Her heart raced beneath his palm, her forehead rested on his, and her short breaths matched his in intensity and need.

"Blue, I'm going to make love to you," he murmured between quick, soft kisses. "Do you understand?"

She nodded, the slightest of movements. Yes, she understood. Her unfathomable need for him was the only thing she did understand about the night. The tawny-haired giant with the beautiful face and the shocking heat in his touch wanted her. She didn't understand the how or why, but she understood the need.

"Right," he drawled with the barest hint of a smile, as if he were reading her mind. "I don't understand that part myself. But I do understand this"—he brushed his thumb across the peak of her breast and watched her oh-so-thick lashes half-close over dark eyes—"and I know I want more, that I want to give you more. That's enough for me tonight . . . if that's enough for you." His voice trailed off with the admission of his doubt. He wasn't used to giving second chances, and the hesitation he felt in her made him wish he hadn't given her an out. "Don't make any rash decisions," he said softly, drawing her closer until his lips rested at the corner of her mouth. "Just kiss me again. Kiss me, Blue, like you did before."

She was incapable of making decisions, especially with his mouth so close to hers. She turned her face a bare inch and found his tongue tasting her lips. Her last shred of reason drowned in a wave of pleasure. She sank against him and melted like sugar in the rain.

Walker gathered her close and melted right along with her, lowering them both to the floor. Then she surprised him again. Suddenly-free hands tunneled through his hair, but he didn't stop her sweet kissing to ask her how she'd unloosened the belt. Instead, he pressed against her, letting her feel the arousal she'd given him, and he kept kissing her, deep and long and slow, savoring her soft moans of desire. It was crazy, the whole thing was crazy, and he never wanted it to end, not until he was deep inside her and her soft moans turned into a cry of release. He'd be with her then, completely.

"Blue," he said with a groan, his voice raw. "Lift your hips." He made his request again, but with a thoroughly different intent. When she hesitated, he moved his mouth to her neck and grazed his teeth up to her ear, gently gnawing a path of destruction on her doubts. "You can say no, Blue. Anytime you want to," he promised, and wondered fleetingly if he meant it. "Do you want to?"

Not when he did that she didn't. He'd started something inside her she didn't know how to finish. Something she didn't know how to run from.

Walker felt her soften beneath him, and he shamelessly pressed his advantage, swirling his tongue through the delicate shell of sensitive skin and sucking on her earlobe. "Lift your hips, sweet Blue. Take off your jeans."

Blue died a little inside at his intimate nibbling and the tenderness in his voice, but when she spoke, she spoke the truth, breathlessly. "I can't."

"Can't?"

"Too scared." And she was, for no reason she could explain any more than she could explain how they'd gotten this far, or what he was doing to her.

She hadn't believed him when he'd used those words, but Walker believed her. He didn't want to, but he did.

"There's nothing to be afraid of, Blue," he said softly. "We're going to make love. You and me. If it'll help, I'll take my jeans off first." He levered himself up on one elbow and reached for the top button on his fly; her hand grabbed his and stopped him. A sharp breath caught in his throat; she was so close to touching him where he needed her to touch him. He slipped his fingers around through hers and held her there for a long, sweetly torturous moment, the slowly raised slumberous eyes to meet hers—and just as slowly moved her hand down the front of his jeans. Sweet, hot pleasure spread through his body and forced his eyes closed. "Take off your jeans, Blue," he growled.

"Walker," she gasped his name, barely making a sound. The raw need in his voice frightened her; the fullness filling her hand excited her, and she couldn't think, couldn't reconcile the two. "This is crazy," she said to herself, unaware she'd spoken aloud.

"I've done crazier," he answered, holding her to him, kissing her brow, her cheeks, and lingering at the corner of her mouth. "Do you want to say no?" She shook her head. "Can you say yes?" She shook her head again, and he let out a deep, pained breath, fighting a silent battle with his hormones, a battle he'd never lost, not when a woman said no. He pushed off her with a groan and sat up with his back against the couch. Squeezing his eyes shut in frustration, he rested his head on the cushions.

Blue watched him force his breathing into a steady rhythm, all of his thoughts and emotions plainly written in the vulnerable expression on his face. He'd been ready to make love, more than ready, and he'd willingly lowered his defenses in anticipation. The act of trust overwhelmed her.

"I'm sorry, Blue," he said softly. "I didn't know you were a virgin." She'd surprised him again. Damn.

"What's that got to do with anything?" she whispered, embarrassed by his assumption.

His amber eyes opened and burned a golden path up her body, before finally meeting her gaze with a wry glint of humor. "Apparently everything." He sighed and dragged a hand through his hair. "Let's not do this again. Okay?"

"Okay," she agreed softly, blushing a rosy hue beneath her tan.

Without taking his eyes off her, he pulled his shirt out of his jeans, his smile fading. When he was covered, he stood up with a slight wince. "Come on. I'll take care of your hand. Then you and the dog better get out of here."

"You're letting me go?"

"At this point, I'm begging you to go," he drawled, walking past her toward the kitchen.

"I'm not going without my map," she warned, struggling to her feet. She'd die of embarrassment later, when she was free.

"You'll go without the map, or you'll go to jail." He picked the map up as he passed the desk and stuffed it in his shirt pocket.

"You won't find anything without me."

"Just make sure I don't find you again." He disappeared into the kitchen. "Get in here, Blue."

The embarrassment refused to wait. She felt the heat racing up her cheeks, and she felt her body pulsing with all the other sensations he'd created out of thin air with his touch. She pushed a hand through her hair and closed her eyes, taking a deep breath. What had gotten into her? She'd never done anything like that in her life.

Walker Evans's kisses got into you, Blue. The answer came easily. *Get out of here while the getting is good.*

"Don't make me come in there after you," he called from the kitchen, sounding completely back in control and so damned sure of himself.

Mortified, she squeezed her eyes closed tighter and shook her head. The last thing she wanted was for him to come after her. "I . . . uh . . . you don't have to fix my hand," she answered. "I've got a first aid kit in my pack."

"And your pack is two miles up the mountain, in the dark, in a beauty of a storm." His voice became clearer, closer. "Even I couldn't find it tonight, and I know where it is."

She opened her eyes and found him lounging against the doorjamb, watching her. He filled the frame with his broad shoulders, lean torso, and long, powerful legs. His clothes were rumpled, his tawny hair tousled—both her fault, she realized with a strange sense of loss. She'd done that to him.

"I'm leaving," she said.

"What's the matter?" he drawled softly, his mouth curving in an easy, mocking smile. "Don't you trust yourself?"

"You're arrogant." She stuffed her shirt back in her jeans, refusing to look at him.

"And you're pretty."

She stopped with her hand half inside her waistband. *Pretty?* Her blush returned, and she silently cursed herself for being a fool. With jerky movements she finished tucking herself together. She looked around at the floor and found her boots and socks next to a chair. She sat down and drew them near.

"Okay, have it your way." He pulled a key chain out of his jeans pocket and unclipped a key. He tossed it over by her. "Take my car. It's not much, but it should get you to wherever you're going. Don't let it be the ranch. They're waiting for you there. Your dog is half dead. Don't stop in Walden, but there's a vet in Steamboat, Andy Marks. Please don't mention my name."

Blue stared at the key lying on the rug, a shiny dab of metal representing her freedom. "You don't have to do this," she whispered.

"Yes I do." Seducing a woman, or at least trying to, and then turning her over to the cops was way out of Walker's league. Sending her out into a high-country storm in the middle of the night with nothing but the shirt on her back and the boots on her feet was also outside his range of possible actions. A few women he'd known would be glad to know he had a few scruples after all.

Hell, now she had him surprising himself, but she'd also brought him the map—which was more than he'd had before.

"They'll think I stole your car."

"If they catch you, and please try and make damn sure they don't, I won't press charges."

"I'll get it back to you."

"If you can. Otherwise don't worry about it. It's not much, and I've got my truck."

Blue nodded and began lacing up her boots, still unable to look up at him.

Walker had the opposite problem. He couldn't stop looking at her. She amazed him, and intrigued him beyond reasonable bounds. He hadn't kissed a virgin since high school, but he didn't remember any of those girls kissing like Blue Dalton. An unsettling thought crossed his mind.

"How old are you?" he asked.

"Old enough."

"To vote? Or to buy a shot and a beer?"

"Both." She tied off one boot and started on the other.

"No boyfriends?" He couldn't imagine any man getting as close as he had tonight and giving up, unless of course the lady made a habit of saying no when she meant yes. Because she'd meant yes. In every way possible she'd said yes—in every way except the one that mattered most.

"I had a boyfriend once, in Texas. *He* was nice," she said defensively, her insinuation clear. Her mouth firmed into a grim line, and she kept on lacing in silence—in, out, tighten; in, out, tighten. When she was finished, she stood up and finally faced him, brushing the hair back off her face. "I'll be back for my map."

"I'll look forward to seeing you again." The grin was back in place, a lazy, sensuous curve of what she now admitted was a very masculine mouth.

"You probably won't see me," she said, tearing her gaze away and glancing around the cabin. "Can I borrow a coat? Mine's still wet."

"Help yourself." He crossed his arms over his chest and nodded at the array of outerwear hanging by the front door.

Blue chose a navy-blue parka. She rolled the sleeves before she put it on, and they still hung past her hips. The coat hung to her knees, reminding her of the lean, hard body it usually shielded from the cold. The heat rose in her again, all through her. She stole a glance at him, unable to stop herself.

"Why don't you bring the car around," he said, grinning lazily, reading the thoughts on her face as clearly as if she'd written "What happened? And can you make it happen again?" on a piece of paper and handed it to him. Trouble, he thought, pure trouble. "The car is in the barn. You can't miss it. I'll carry the dog, if he'll—" He jerked his head toward the kitchen and a second later swore under his breath.

The look on his face frightened her like nothing in his touch had. Then she saw a flash of red light streak across the cabin wall.

"Take off the coat," he commanded. "Get back on the couch."

"No!" She lunged for the door. She was too close to freedom to lose now.

He caught her as her hand wrapped around the doorknob. "Dammit, Blue." He hauled her back against his chest, lifting her feet off the floor and swinging her around. "You'll never make it. Ouch! Dammit! Don't fight me!" He hefted her higher, getting his arm out of reach of her teeth. "So help me God, if you bite me again, I'll—" The sound of slamming car doors stopped him in mid-sentence.

Blue twisted her head around, her eyes wide

with fear. "Hide me, Walker," she pleaded. "I swear I'll—"

"Hush, Blue," he interrupted, crossing to the couch. "You swear too much, and there's no place to hide you in here. Let me do the talking. Give me the coat."

He dropped her on the couch, and she slipped her arms out of the sleeves. "Don't give me up, please . . . please."

Her fear affected him the same way her tears had; it made him feel helpless, worse than helpless. It made him feel the failures of the years. There had been a time when the Evans name had been worth special considerations in these parts, but no longer, not since his father had run the ranch into the ground. They were coming to get her, and there wasn't a damn thing he could do about it.

"You have to go with them tonight," he told her, ignoring the pounding on the door. "But I'll come for you tomorrow. I promise."

She looked up at him with her dark eyes, her mouth trembling. "Why?" Confusion turned the word into a whisper.

"I don't know," he said honestly, but he knew he would.

"Walker! Are you in there?"

"Open up, Evans!"

"Maybe because I need you." He pushed the map lower in his shirt pocket and attempted a smile.

"It's mine." A bit of the fight came back into her eyes, assuring him she hadn't given up, not yet.

"We'll see. Don't worry, Blue. The Jackson County jail isn't as bad as some." His smile spread into a grin, deepening the creases in his too-perfect face.

"And you've seen a few I'll bet." A weak smile touched the corner of her mouth.

Walker wanted to say something dumb, like "That's my girl," but she was far from being anybody's girl. Blue Dalton was one of a kind. She was scared and trying not to show it. She'd cried over having shot a man, but she'd shot the man who'd needed it. She'd outmaneuvered him in all ways, except the one that counted, resorting to kisses when violence had failed—and he doubted if she'd given an ounce of thought to either set of actions. The lady ran on instinct, something he recognized from personal experience as a sure way to get into trouble, and a pretty good way of getting back out with your skin intact but with little else.

"Evans! We're coming in!"

He held her gaze a moment longer and made his promise once more. "I'll come for you, Blue."

She nodded, and he watched a mask of indifference fall across her face, hiding the fears he knew were still there. He wanted to touch her again, but he held back.

"Walker! You better open up this door!"

"Hold your horses, Bowles," he hollered. "I'm coming."

He strode across the cabin, opened the door, and all hell broke loose. The posse swarmed into his living room, guns drawn.

"She's unarmed," he growled, his anger flaring at the stupid, macho display. He glared at Bowles. "Tell them to back off!"

Bowles shrugged. "It's their show, Walker."

"Shut up, pretty boy. Or I'll get you for aiding and abetting." The sheriff pushed by him. "On your feet, Dalton. Get up against the wall and spread 'em. Taggart, search the place."

"You bastard." Walker acted without thinking, grabbing the sheriff's arm and jerking him back. He towered over the shorter man, but that didn't stop the sheriff's threats.

"Touch me again, and I'll have you up on assault." He pulled free, and Walker let him go, but not without a threat of his own.

"Touch her, and I'll give you a reason."

"Cool it, Walker. He's just doing his job." Bowles stepped between the two men. The sheriff moved over to Blue. Lower, under his breath, Bowles said, "You should have radioed in the minute you found her. This looks bad, real bad, the two of you sitting around all cozylike. The sheriff figured you were up to something. Dammit, Walker. I told him we could trust you."

Walker clenched his fists at his sides. Bowles was right, but that didn't make watching Blue any easier. Her mask was slipping. She bit down on her lower lip when the sheriff kicked her feet apart, and she squeezed her eyes shut as his hands patted down her body. He was efficient, though, and quick, and all too soon he had her cuffed and heading for the door.

Taggart came out of the kitchen holding the two rifles. "Which one is hers?"

"The Winchester," Walker snapped, not taking his eyes off Blue.

"Where's the rest of her stuff?"

"Her coat is by the door. I had to leave her backpack up on the mountain."

"This it?" the sheriff asked, picking out the smallest jacket.

"Yes," Walker said. "But she can't wear that one. It's wet." He lifted the navy-blue parka off the couch and came up behind Blue. He draped the coat over her shoulders, but her shoulders were too small to hold it up by themselves. Swearing softly, he stepped in front of her and pulled the front panels together. He got the first two buttons fastened before he gave up on his own macho display. His gaze lifted, slowly meeting hers, and the fear in her eyes reached way down deep inside him, branding him with their shared defeat.

He buttoned the next two buttons without looking, lowering his head to whisper in her ear so very softly, "I'll come for you, Blue. You can count on it."

He felt her trembling inside the coat and swore to himself. Then he stepped back and watched them take her away.

Four

He wasn't coming. She was a fool to think he would come. And even if he did come, there wasn't anything he could do for her—except give her back the map.

Blue knotted her hands in her lap and continued staring at the beige wall of her cell. He'd had all day to come, and he hadn't. Maybe it was better if he didn't come. Dammit! She tightened her hands until her knuckles went white. What was she going to do?

She hadn't made her one phone call yet.

"With good reason," she muttered under her breath. Who was she going to call? Her aunt and uncle in Galveston? That would go over like a ton of bricks. They'd always thought Abel's side of the family was a lot on the disreputable side, and she'd never been able to fault their opinion.

"Talking to yourself again, Blue?" The deputy named Taggart stopped by her cell and leaned against the bars, grinning from ear to ear. "You know what they say, don't you? Then again, maybe you're setting yourself up for a plea of insanity." He pushed off the bars and chuckled. "Keep talking, Blue. Just keep on a-talking. Maybe you'll talk yourself down to manslaughter, that's if the old coot ever kicks off."

Jerk, she thought, not bothering to look at him. She'd seen enough of the yahoo to tide her over until she was ninety. The man she'd shot, O'Keefe they called him, wasn't going to die. She'd heard the officers talking about him, and he'd been in trouble with the law long before he'd been in trouble with her. All of her tears and awful fears had been for nothing except for more trouble in Walker Evans's arms, a man she was unlikely to ever see again—*along with her map.*

She covered her eyes with one hand and rested her elbow on her thigh. What was she going to do? The walls were closing in on her, making it hard to breathe. She wrapped her other arm around her waist and began rocking slowly back and forth on the cot. Her fingers gripped her shirt. What were they trying to do? she wondered in anger, cook her? Sweat ran down her sides and between her breasts. Her face was hot and her mind was racing around in circles. She wiped her cheek with her shoulder.

Claustrophobia, she thought. *That's what you've got, not heat prostration. Don't think about it.*

"Sure," she said aloud, and immediately wished she hadn't. Maybe she was going crazy. If Walker Evans would walk through the door right now and get her out of there, she'd let him have the map, a sure sign of insanity in her book.

• • •

"Can't you hurry up, David?"

"Let me handle this, Walker. You've had me running my tail off since midnight." David stopped and checked his Rolex, then went back to signing papers. "You're going to be in debt to me for the rest of your life."

"I'll just jack the price up the next time you bring all those Seventeenth Avenue dudes up for their annual dose of machismo."

"They're lawyers, not dudes, and they come for relaxation, not machismo. John wants a trophy trout this year, or he's not coming back." David flipped a page and ran his finger down the lines.

"Tell him to spend more time on his casting and less money on his equipment. I think his cane rod scares off my plebeian fish."

"Right." David laughed and continued checking his papers. "Your sister told me not to come home without pinning you down on a date for a visit and dinner."

"Anytime." The sheer bulk of the papers impressed Walker. The one thing he'd learned about the law was that if you were ever in trouble with it, you'd better put everything you had, your money, your faith, and your future, in the hands of the most heartless lawyer you could find and afford. David wasn't much of a fisherman, but he was a real tough lawyer. That David was also the closest thing he had to a brother didn't sway Walker's opinion in the least about the man's legal skills.

"Can you do it? Can you get her out tonight?"

David glanced up at the door leading to the sheriff's office, then back to Walker. A lean smile graced his face. "As soon as he opens his door, I'm going to be all over him like a vulture on dead meat. He's got no case, and he knows it. O'Keefe confessed to cutting her with his knife. The doctor says the only thing he's ever going to die from is old age or a pickled liver. He's got a rap sheet a mile long, and as soon as your sheriff is through with him, the boys in Topeka will have him extradited. Annabelle Dalton won't have to worry about him again. She did leave the scene of the crime, but you told me she was scared. I'll use it if the judge has a problem."

"Do you think there's going to be a problem?" Walker didn't like the sounds of any more problems cropping up.

"No," David replied. "She's pure as the driven snow. She owns the Jeep, her firearm is registered, even her credit is good. There'll be a fine for diving in the lake. You could press trespassing charges, but I doubt if you'll be doing that."

"No." Walker smiled, his first smile since last night. "I won't be pressing charges."

"Mr. London? Sheriff Johnson will see you now." One of the deputies came out of the office door, holding it open.

David grinned and picked up his briefcase. "This is going to cost you a fortune, Walker."

Walker grinned back. "It's worth a fortune."

"Up on your feet, Blue. You've got a visitor." Taggart jangled his key ring as he walked down the hall. "Your pretty boy came to see you. Bet that makes you real glad."

What's he jabbering about now? Blue wondered.

She didn't know any pretty boys, and if she had, she wasn't at all sure she'd own up to it.

"Come on, honey. You've been sprung. That's some kind of lawyer you've got. He just ran over my boss like a Mack truck. Haven't seen Johnson that steamed since . . . since I don't know when." Taggart laughed and fitted the key into the lock.

Now he had her attention. Blue grabbed her coat and swallowed the dregs of a cold cup of coffee left over from supper. She didn't know any pretty boys, and she sure as hell didn't have a lawyer, but if dumb old Taggart was going to open her cell door, she was going to be out of there before he could spit or change his mind.

"Slow down, honey. I've got to check you out before you can leave."

"You've done all the checking you're going to, and don't call me honey." She shouldered past him and immediately felt a weight lift off her heart, and a hand grab her arm.

"Slow down. I'm talking about those two nickels you had in your pocket. Don't want the citizenry thinking we steal from you felons when we get you in here."

"I'm not a felon."

"Well, you're not exactly the Queen of England either."

"Never claimed to be." She shook free of his hand.

He grabbed her shoulder instead and pushed her in front of him through a door. "You're a real cuss, Blue, just like your old man. I sure hope Walker knows what he's got himself into."

Blue stopped cold in her tracks, and Taggart bumped into her. She whirled around, half coming out of her coat. "Walker Evans?" The weight on her heart came crashing back down, but differently, more jumpy, less heavy, but no less scary. She'd convinced herself he wasn't coming, and she wasn't ready to face him again. She'd never be ready after last night.

"What's the holdup, Taggart?" a deep voice asked, and Blue cringed inside. Darn him, he walked as softly as he talked.

"I don't know, Walker. I don't think the lady wants to go with you."

"Sure she does. Don't you, Blue?"

The question was moot. In truth, she'd go with anybody to get out of there, even if it meant swallowing the last of her pride and looking at Walker Evans. She did both, carefully, slowly.

Walker met her gaze straight on, without any of the hesitation he saw in her eyes. "Get her things," he said to Taggart, still watching Blue. She looked worse than when he'd found her. Her hair was limp and tangled, her expression more closed, without a hint of the sweetness he'd found in her kiss. Pale-blue smudges below her eyes bespoke of her lack of sleep. Lines of strain around her mouth told him she'd been thinking too hard and too fast.

"How's my dog?" she asked, and he could see the effort it cost her. A small muscle twitched in her jaw. She looked ready to jump out of her skin. He knew the feeling; he hadn't liked jail either.

"I had the vet come out to the house to check him over. He took a stitch or two, but he's fine," he assured her.

"Thanks for taking care of him. He's . . . he's a

good dog. The best." Dark-brown eyes met his for a second before she looked away again.

Taggart returned with a manila envelope and her rifle. "Here's your stuff. You'll have to sign for everything." He started to hand them both to her, but Walker intercepted the rifle, his hand closing around the barrel just above hers. She didn't look at him this time, but her hand tightened and pulled. He pulled harder and reached down with his other hand and pried her fingers loose.

"We're doing this my way."

She knew she was no match for him. With a muttered curse she released the gun. Angry but compliant, she checked the contents of the envelope and scrawled her name across the clipboard Taggart held out. Walker had gotten her out of jail. She'd let him hold the rifle if he wanted to, until she was out of the place. But the minute she breathed fresh air, she was going to set him straight about a lot of things, including her map. Her moment of insanity had passed.

"Been real nice having you, Miss Dalton," Taggart teased. "You're welcome back anytime."

Her reply shocked the smile off the deputy's face and brought one to Walker's. The lady sure likes playing with fire, he thought, grinning broadly, but her mouth needs a good soaping.

"Come on, Blue. Let's get out of here before Taggart loses his sense of humor." He turned and walked toward the door, confident she would follow but listening for her footsteps nonetheless.

He stopped at the door and held it open for her. She slipped by him, obvious in her attempt not to touch him. He didn't blame her. He hadn't exactly cast himself in the role of the noble hero. They both knew why he'd come for her, and it had more to do with Dalton's Treasure than the craziness in front of the fireplace, or so he'd been telling himself for the last twenty-four hours. Looking at her, he didn't know what had caused him to kiss her in the first place. She wasn't the type who usually brought kissing to mind. With his coat hanging past her knees, and her rolled-up jeans, she resembled a bag lady.

Outside, David waited by his silver Mercedes, drinking coffee out of a Styrofoam cup.

With a touch of his hand Walker guided her toward the car. "There's someone who wants to meet you." Blue took one look and balked, but Walker kept pushing.

"Let go of me, you—"

"Play nice, Blue. Don't bite," Walker whispered, tightening his grip. Louder, he said, "Blue, I'd like you to meet your lawyer, David London. He drove all the way up from Denver to get you out tonight."

"Thanks," she said, not sounding in the least as though she meant it. She tried again to pull away from him. Walker held her tighter.

"Miss Dalton," David said, extending his hand. Blue ignored the gesture, and he let his hand drop back to his side. "Do you have any questions?" Walker noted the exchange and added etiquette lessons to his list of what Blue Dalton needed.

"How much are you costing me?" she asked point-blank.

The figure the lawyer named slackened her jaw. She stared at him, dumbfounded. Then her gaze drifted over the Mercedes, back to his cashmere coat, and slowly up to Walker's face. "Thanks a lot."

"You're welcome," he said, nonplussed by her sarcasm.

"The man you shot is recovering without complications," David continued. "You can pick up your Jeep as soon as you get a new set of tires. If you'd like to press charges, I'll be happy to represent you."

"What kind of charges?" she grumbled, more intent on freeing herself than listening to an outrageously expensive lawyer she couldn't afford. The man at her back was having none of it, though; his one hand held her in a grip she couldn't break without causing a scene.

"Attempted rape," David said.

Blue slanted an angry glance at Walker. "He never laid a hand on me," she said between gritted teeth. "I shot him before he had the chance."

Walker took the words and the flash in her eyes as fair warning, and he took them as a challenge.

"Assault?" David offered.

Blue shifted her gaze to the lawyer. "He nicked me and I shot him. Now who do you think got the wrong end of the assault?" She didn't want to get balled up in a court case over a knife cut, not when the man was already going to jail. She'd dished out her dose of justice in the cabin, and she'd learned her lesson. From now on she'd make sure no one backed her into a corner.

"How about destruction of property? Your tires."

"Hiring you would probably cost me more than buying a new set," she said bluntly.

"Yes . . . well, then I guess we've covered everything." David coughed discreetly into his hand, hiding a smile. "Walker knows how to get in touch with me if you have any other questions."

"What about theft?" she asked.

The high-priced lawyer looked at her, then up at Walker. "There wasn't anything about a theft in the report."

Walker was going to strangle her. All he had to do was decide whether to do it now, in front of David, or wait until he got her alone. "There wasn't any theft," he said, sliding his hand across Blue's shoulders in warning.

Dark-brown eyes met his steadily. "Easy for you to say. You're the one who sto—"

He whipped her around, muffling her words against his coat as he hugged the daylights out of her. "Lord, I missed you, Blue. Let's go home, darlin', and let David get back to Denver. We've got so much to talk about." He squeezed her tighter and sidestepped the kick he felt coming. He cupped her head in his palm, keeping her face buried against his chest. "David, thanks a lot for coming." He winced as she landed a boot on his shin.

"Walker?"

Ignoring the confusion on David's face, Walker tightened his grip around her waist and in one smooth move hefted her over his shoulder, knocking the breath out of her for the seconds he needed. "She's mad. I was late." He backed off a step. "I was supposed to pick her up early this morning. You know how women get." Walker was sure he'd heard weaker excuses, but he couldn't remember when.

Luckily, David accepted the explanation, not because he was easily fooled, which Walker knew he wasn't, but probably because he was tired. Then again, anyone who lived with his sister had to be pretty well versed in the vagaries of the female mind, and anyone who didn't know Blue Dalton wouldn't know the usual female vagaries didn't apply.

He saw David cast a curious glance at the woman grappling in his arms. Walker hefted her again to keep her quiet, knocking the breath out of her as gently as possible. "Thanks for helping us out," he said by way of good-bye.

"Good luck." David gave up with a shrug and slid into the plush leather seat of the Mercedes. Before he closed the door, he glanced up and nodded at Blue. "You're going to need it." A moment later he drove off.

Blue found her breath and her voice the same instant the Mercedes purred to life. "Put . . . put me down!" She tried to free her legs and found his hold unbreakable. "I'm warning you, Walker Evans! You've got more nerve than is healthy!"

"Spare me the idle threats." He started walking toward his truck, taking long strides, and trying not to bounce her on his shoulder. "Have you ever heard of the word gratitude?"

"Gra-gratitude? For wh-what? B-breaking my ribs?" Blue knew what he wanted, and she'd be damned if she'd give it to him. Not when he was hauling her around like a sack of flour.

"I'm sure you can come up with a reason if you put your mind to it. Or do you want me to leave you here where Taggart can find you and pick you up for vagrancy?"

"Talk about idle threats!"

Walker opened the driver's-side door and dumped her inside. "Scoot over," he ordered, getting in next to her after he slipped her rifle behind the seat.

"Where are you taking me?" She moved as far away from him as the truck cab allowed.

"Home."

"Good," she said with a huff, staring out the windshield. She could put up with him for another hour.

"Not the North Star, Blue. You're going home with me."

"The hell I am."

"Woman"—he sighed, gripping the steering wheel with both hands—"you're pushing your luck, and it ran out twenty-four hours ago."

"About the same time yours did, *pretty boy*." The words were out before she gave them the thought she should have.

Her quick glance proved the mistake. She'd never seen anyone get so angry so quietly. His hands twisted around the steering wheel, his jaw went tight, but neither action compared to the cold hardness in his eyes. Bright glints of steel bore down on her across the dark cab, sending a nervous tremor through her heart. Her hand slid to the catch on the door, ready for the fast escape she knew she'd need if he gave in to his silent fury.

His gaze went to her hand, and his eyes darkened another degree. "Don't even think it, Blue." He turned the key and jammed the truck into gear.

She grabbed the door handle as he wheeled the truck in reverse out of the parking spot.

"Buckle up." He slammed on the brakes and checked the street both ways before shoving the gearshift up into first. "There's one thing you better get straight in your mind." He quelled her with a long, hard look, his face grim. "I won't take that pretty boy crap off of you, ever. Remember that, Blue. I won't tell you twice." He stepped on the gas, and the wheels kicked up gravel as they took off into the mountains and the night.

Blue wanted to breathe a sigh of relief—she knew she'd gotten off easy—but the easy breath wouldn't come. She was still in the mountain lion's den, and the lion was bigger and faster and stronger than she was. She hoped to high heaven she'd prove to be smarter.

Forty minutes later his quietness and the rattletrap shimmy of the truck had worn down her patience to a frayed edge and her anger to a dull throb.

"You lied to me," she said, breaking the silence before it broke her.

Walker thought about her statement for a minute, then said, "A couple of times, but I didn't think you'd noticed."

"When?" She cast him a curious glance. She hadn't expected him to agree so easily with her insult.

"Why don't you tell me which lie you're talking about first."

"Jail. Either you've never been in one, or you've got a twisted sense of what's bad and what isn't."

"I didn't lie. I've been in the old Jackson County jail twice. I figured the new one had to be better."

"Well, the new one looked pretty old to me. What were you? A juvenile delinquent?"

He shifted his weight in the seat, not bothering

to reply, but Blue wasn't going to be put off that easily.

"What did they get you on? Kidnapping? Or theft?" Both options were high on her list of complaints against Walker Evans—very high.

He slanted her a dry look, then went back to watching the road. After a while he said, "I got in a couple of fights."

"Must have been pretty bad ones. I never knew anybody to get thrown in jail for a little one."

He shrugged and kept driving.

"You must have broken something," she said, following her train of thought out loud. "Something . . . or somebody." Her train of thought ran into a brick wall, and her voice trailed off. She'd been angry with him since he'd tracked her down on the mountain, but she'd never been truly afraid of him, and this was a distinctly inopportune moment to start.

From beneath her lashes she glanced in his direction. He had a rugged profile, made up of shadows and angles softened only by the length of his hair. A slight crease in his cheek attested to more years in the sun and the wind than she'd previously attributed to him, years enough for him to have learned the wilier ways of getting what he wanted out of life. What did she really know about him?

As if drawn by her doubts, his gaze met hers across the dim interior of the truck.

"Okay, Blue," he drawled softly. "You can quit thinking so hard. You're fogging the windshield. I was sixteen the first time I landed in jail. I caught one of my father's poker buddies hanging around my little sister's bedroom. It's true, I tried to kill him, but I was kind of skinny at sixteen, and all I managed was to break his nose before he broke my arm." He saw her eyes grow wider, and he would have stopped, except he didn't want any more of those kinds of problems cropping up between them. He needed her trust not her fear to find Lacey's Lode. "The second time I was nineteen. No excuses that time. I was drunk, my father was drunk, and I guess we'd pretty much had it with each other. We tore up the bar in Gould and as much of each other as we could get a handhold on. Satisfied?"

Shocked was more like it. She lowered her gaze to her hands in her lap and pressed her lips together. Her own childhood hadn't been much better, but she'd grown up thinking everyone else lived normally. Walker Evans hadn't, though. The similarity in circumstances disconcerted her, made her resentment harder to hold on to.

Walker felt her shying away, and he sighed deeply, lifting one hand off the steering wheel in a gesture of resignation. "I don't know what else I can tell you, except if I was inclined to hurt you, last night would have been a prime opportunity."

"That's . . . that's not what I meant. It's just that, well, I fought with my father a lot, too, but we . . . we never—"

"Good," he interrupted her. "A man who abuses a woman ought to be shot, but I guess you already figured that out for yourself."

"I didn't want to shoot him," she said softly.

"And I already figured that out. Don't worry, Blue. You did the right thing." He looked over at her and was struck once again by her delicacy. The dashboard lights caught the slight upturn of her nose, the gentle curves of her brow and cheek-bones, and the worried frown tightening her full mouth. Suddenly he found himself feeling the same cold anger he'd felt at sixteen when Ralston had stood at the foot of Janelle's bed and watched her sleep. "Listen to me, Blue. Every time you feel guilty, I want you to remember one thing. O'Keefe wanted to break you into a thousand different pieces, inside and out. You were smart enough and quick enough to stop him. That's control, and you took it. The only problem I've got with what you did is that you missed, but in the long run that's probably better for your peace of mind. In the same situation I wouldn't have been as generous."

"I tried to shoot you too," she reluctantly reminded him, glancing up.

"And missed again, thank God." He flashed her a quick grin. "I'm beginning to wonder why you carry a rifle."

"I usually don't miss, Walker. That's the truth. I guess my nerves were frazzled."

"Considering that you passed out when I grabbed you, I'd guess your guess is a pretty good one."

"Then you're not holding a grudge?"

Walker let his grin slip into a sly smile and captured her gaze with his own. "Not about what happened on the mountain," he drawled, his voice silky smooth, leaving no doubts in her mind about what he meant.

Blue shifted uneasily in her seat. She wished he wouldn't look at her like that, as if he knew more about what she was thinking than she did, because suddenly what she found herself thinking was way out of line. It had something to do with his mouth and maybe his eyes—and the enforced intimacy of the truck cab. She was definitely out of line.

Taggart was wrong about him. He wasn't pretty, not with his square jaw, not with those shoulders and those hands, and not with that wolfish gleam in his eyes.

Every predator needed its prey, and she instinctively knew which role she'd been cast in. Walker was no O'Keefe; he didn't want to break her. He wanted to consume her. For the life of her she couldn't imagine why, but she'd felt it last night in his kiss, and she saw it now in the night-darkened depths of his eyes.

He wasn't for her, any fool could have seen the fact. She didn't know why the possibility even crossed her mind. Men like him were for prettier women who knew how to play the mating game—a game, if last night was any indication, he had mastered long ago. She still didn't believe what had happened to her when he'd kissed her, how warm and soft his skin had felt beneath her fingers, the hard angles of his face, the softness of his hair falling over her hands, the tautness and the sheer masculine power of his body as he'd drawn her close and held her as if he'd never let her go. He'd intoxicated her with his strength and the gentle way he'd yielded it to her with his kiss. She remembered cupping his jaw with her hand and feeling his mouth shift and open and close over hers, the tightening of the muscles when he'd sucked her tongue into his mouth, the ensuing relaxation when he'd released her to trace her lips. She remembered too much.

He slowed the truck, and the barest beginnings

of panic caught on the edges of her emotions. She looked out the window, recognized his cabin, and knew she should have fought harder in front of the jail, map or no map. Staying with him was like jumping out of the frying pan into the fire; she was bound to get burned.

Five

Blue stood in the middle of his living room, her mouth agape, staring at him with a mixture of disbelief and horror. She had one hand wrapped around her pack strap and the other holding on to her dog.

"You wh-what?" she stammered.

"I memorized it and burned it," he repeated, leaning back against the moss rock mantel of the fireplace. He shoved his hands into the front pockets of his jeans, carefully watching her from what he hoped was a safe distance. "You're stuck with me. We either work together, or we both end up with nothing."

Stuck with him? Nothing? Blue took a long, trembling breath, trying to control the anger she felt building inside. He'd burned her map. Burned it! Despite her assertive declaration to the contrary the previous night, her life had been up for grabs in the icy black waters of Lake Agnes.

"Do you . . . have . . . know . . . what I—" she

sputtered, words failing her. She needed to sit down before her knees buckled. The backpack fell to the floor with a thump, and Trapper backed off. She made her way over to the couch and dropped into the corner, clenching her fists in her lap. Frustration lowered her chin to her chest.

Leaving was out of the question. Everything she needed, everything she'd worked for had disappeared inside his head. His *pretty* head, she thought, silently daring him to read her mind and do something about it.

Walker shifted uneasily on his feet, moving his weight from one hip to the other, more than a little amazed at her ability to make him nervous. He'd never known a woman to do it with such unsubtle skill, but if looks could kill, she'd have him on his knees.

"Of course, you do have one other option," he said, trying not to grin at himself or, heaven forbid, at her. The lady was in no mood to be teased.

"Forget it," she snapped, and walked away, knowing full well what he meant. She'd be damned if she gave him the starting mark. For one night, and given no choice, she'd trusted him with her map. During all those hours in jail she'd convinced herself she'd be able to get it back from him. Well, the mountain lion had outsmarted her, but he was a long way from finding Dalton's Treasure . . . *from finding Lacey's Lode.*

The thought came out of her subconscious, pushing her anger aside with the glimmer of a new plan. She slowly raised her gaze, measuring him from the toes of his boots to the golden-brown depths of his eyes. He was big, and he was too good-looking by a long shot with his rogue's face and tawny mane of hair—as if God had decided just once to try for perfection in a mortal man—but Walker hadn't won, not yet.

"I'll give you half the gold I find if you'll give me the directions from the map," she stated her double-crossing proposition without a shred of guilt. Treasure hunting had never been a game for the fainthearted.

"Well, that's a helluva deal, Blue," he drawled, the lazy gleam coming back into his eyes. "I'll make you the same offer and do you one better."

Blue blushed under his assessing gaze, and her voice took on a wary tone. "What do you mean?"

"If you'll tell me the starting mark, I'll give you all the gold I find, every ounce, every gram, every fleck of color."

She held his eyes, ignoring the jump in her pulse, and slowly said, "That's an awful lot of gold to be giving away."

"It's an awful lot of nothing. There isn't any gold, and you know it." He gave a careless shrug of his shoulders, releasing her by glancing away, and pushed off the mantel. "Now you know I know it too."

Impossible, she thought. He was bluffing. There was no way on earth he could know what lay somewhere beneath the high country of the North Star. The existence of Lacey's Lode was information shared solely between her and the lawyer who had read her father's will. No one else knew the name or the Bible reference Abel had instructed her to find, and not even the lawyer knew what she'd found tucked between the yellowed pages of the King James. Every man who'd ever dogged her trail had been looking for gold, piles of it, pounds of it.

*Every man except this one, Blue. Every man
except for the one who caught you.*

Walker knelt by the hearth and picked up a few
sticks of kindling, giving her a minute to absorb
his words. He'd accomplished his main objective;
he'd stopped her from leaving. The rest was details.

Of course, she wasn't going to like the details
any better than she'd liked him burning her map.
He stopped stacking and stared at the small pieces
of wood in his hand. She probably wouldn't believe him even if he did tell her everything, but he
didn't see any other way; as it stood, she thought
he was a thief. He finished off the pile of kindling
with a couple of logs, then struck a match up the
thigh of his jeans.

When the fire caught, he rested his forearm on
his knee and glanced over his shoulder at her.
Her eyes were downcast, her brow furrowed in
thought. She's a strange one all right, he thought,
warier than the big bucks he tracked in autumn,
more evasive than the trophy trout people paid
him to find, wilder than both and prettier than
either. She was a woman to be reckoned with,
coming into his life at a time when he'd quit
reckoning with anyone.

Her hair slid down the side of her cheek, and
she brushed it back with an impatient gesture.
She looked too young to be a worthy adversary,
but in this case he knew looks were absolutely
deceiving. She more than matched him in stubbornness, and she outmatched any woman he'd
ever met in her contrary effect on him. He wanted
her and didn't want her at the same time. He
understood the wanting. It was the holding back
that had kept him awake half the night. In retro-

spect, he realized he could have convinced her to make love with him and also not to regret the decision. She was just naive enough to buy a good, solid line of persistence, or so he'd told himself in the dark hours before dawn when sleep had been elusive and the memory of her body moving over his hadn't been nearly elusive enough.

Incredible, he thought, watching her, feeling the subtle changes taking place inside himself even though she was across the room. *You better be damn careful, Walker,* he warned himself. *Or you're going to end up in over your head.* He stood up and brushed his hands together, removing the last traces of wood dust.

"Look, Blue, I think things will go smoother if we're straight with each other."

"What . . . things?" she asked, glancing up at him.

"Us working together."

Blue looked at him long and hard, still not sure what to think about his last revelation. Seconds passed one after the other, until she came to the only sensible decision available.

"I'm not working with you," she stated emphatically. "You stole my map and burned it, and unless you give me the directions, I'm going to call that lawyer back and have you arrested. We'll see how well *you* like the new Jackson County jail."

Walker didn't put it past her, for all the good it would do her. "You'll have better luck calling Sheriff Johnson. He's always willing to think the worst of me. David, on the other hand, is my brother-in-law, and my sister, Janelle, would have him skinned and hung out to dry if he brought charges against me."

Great, Blue thought, tightening her jaw in frustration. Her luck was holding true, and it was all bad.

He held her angry gaze for a moment, then headed for the kitchen. "Would you like some coffee while you're thinking up your next move?"

Blue watched him disappear through the doorway, not bothering to give him the reply he hadn't bothered to wait for. Coffee wouldn't help her think her way out of his neat trap, and she never drank anything stronger.

Damn! She was running out of options. The chances of her calling Sheriff Johnson for anything were slim and none. He probably wouldn't be any more inclined to help her than she was to ask him for help. What she'd said to Taggart was nothing compared to the names she'd called Johnson when he'd shoved her into her cell.

But who would have believed Walker's sister had married into such wealth? Her gaze roamed over the well-worn furniture in his small cabin: the leather chair by the fire that looked as if three or four generations of Evans's had enjoyed its softly tanned comfort; the dining table next to the south wall, with its kick-scarred chairs conjuring up impatient little boys in cowboy boots; the handmade curtains hanging at the windows. His brother-in-law's car cost more than the whole kit and caboodle, many times over.

"What have you decided, Blue?" His deep voice drew her head around. "Do we work together? Or do we call it quits?"

"I'll find another lawyer."

"You need a case first, and you don't have one. You and I are the only ones who knew about the map." He crossed the living room and sat down in the leather chair, very close to where she sat on the couch. He set her cup on the end table between them.

Not quite, she thought. "O'Keefe knows."

She was going to wear him out, Walker thought, exhaling a deep breath. She was damn close to doing it already. Every time he thought he had her corralled, she came up with something new. The woman's mind never stopped working overtime. Never. He relaxed back into the chair, not at all sure how much longer his luck would hold. Blue Dalton might well be the end of him. The lady pulled on him, with her dark eyes and fawn-colored skin, with her undeniable courage and the memory of her touch.

Blue watched as he began shaking his head slowly from side to side, his mouth lifting in a disturbingly sensual smile. "You're really something special, Blue," he drawled. "For all the trouble you've been, I wouldn't have missed tangling with you for the world." He stretched his long legs out on the rug and lifted his mug in salute before taking a sip.

Blue stiffened at the mellow timbre of his voice and his smile. He was making fun of her again.

"Save your line of bull, pret—" She stopped herself in the nick of time, her eyes widening in awareness of what she'd almost said.

He acknowledged her quick reconsideration with a grin. "And you're smart, too smart to think dragging O'Keefe into our personal problems is a good idea." It was the only argument he had against her latest threat.

"We don't have a personal problem," she countered.

"Oh, I don't know, Blue. By my figuring, we've got more than one."

"Then you and I are figuring differently."

"Probably," he agreed, though his grin said otherwise. "But then I haven't forgotten how you kissed me last night, and it's real easy to see you're doing your darnedest to try."

He was much too close and much too confident to be saying such things to her. She doubted if she could control the confidence, but putting some distance between them was well within her abilities. She did it without even attempting to disguise the fact, moving to the other end of the couch and taking her coffee with her. His low chuckle followed her retreat.

"We're going to have a hard time finding our fortune if you keep running away from me, Blue."

"You're being awfully generous with *my* fortune," she muttered, keeping her eyes trained on the fire, thinking of how her map had disappeared in the flames, turning to ashes in the grate. She'd worked too hard, sweated out too many years in Texas to lose her inheritance to some no good, backwoods con man.

She flicked a hesitant glance at him. Impossible, she thought again. She couldn't work with him, not when he rattled her concentration just by being in the same room, just by existing in her world. He was too . . . tricky, she decided, avoiding the other descriptive words crowding her brain, dangerous words like magnetic and intriguing.

And she was still thinking too hard, Walker thought, watching her worry herself into a hole from which he'd left her no escape. Two days ago he'd had no intention of sharing the treasure.

Sometime last night, after they'd taken her away, well after he'd kissed her, he'd changed his mind. How much of his decision rested on their fathers' ill-fated partnership and the information she had, and how much of it rested strictly on the mystery of Blue, he didn't know, but the next time he kissed her, he intended to find out. She could run all she wanted; he was more inclined to face the facts. Maybe if she had a few more of those to work with, she wouldn't be so skittish.

"How long have you been looking for your fortune, Blue?" he asked.

"Long enough to have gotten this close."

"He didn't make it easy for you, did he?"

She turned and looked at him, wondering what he was getting at. "He wasn't an easy man," she said.

"Disillusioned men never are, especially after they start drinking."

Blue's hackles rose at his insinuation. More than once, and usually in the heat of anger, she'd called her father a drunk. But she'd never let anybody else get away with it. "You don't know what you're talking about."

The subtle lift of his eyebrow and the wry look he gave her called her a liar. "Haven't you ever wondered why he went to so much trouble to hide what he found?"

Only about a million times. But what Abel rambled on about when he'd been drinking was a far sight different than what he'd admit sober. It wasn't until she'd read his will that she'd finally been convinced there was something to his wild, vague stories. Five years of searching had strengthened her conviction, five years and five run-ins with men like Walker Evans. The others may have been wrong about the gold, but they hadn't doubted the existence of something up there in the hills.

"If you haven't, then you better start," he continued, "and if you run short of answers, you can always ask me. I've got some real good ones when it comes to your father."

"You didn't know my father."

"No," he admitted. "But I knew my father, and he knew Abel better than was good for him."

Riddles. The man was playing with her with his half-spoken intimations. "You've got a funny way of being straight. If you've got something to say, why don't you just say it?"

He leaned forward and rested his elbows on his knees, his hands wrapped around his coffee mug. "Okay, Blue," he said softly. "You tell me when you've heard enough."

Suddenly Blue wished she hadn't asked. His smile had faded, along with the teasing warmth in his eyes. Firelight traced a pattern across his still features, catching a feathering of crow's-feet she hadn't noticed before, highlighting the uncompromising angle of his jaw and the dark stubble of a day's growth of beard. Sable lashes shadowed the weariness in his eyes.

"Your great-grandfather followed the gold rush to Colorado back in the eighteen hundreds," he began slowly, looking up at her. "Unlike most, the trip paid off for him. He struck it rich with the Sweet Mary mine way up in the Sawatch Range. Gold, more than most people can imagine, ran through his claim and through his fingers like water in a river. The only smart investment he made was in the North Star. Ranching has always been more work than payoff, though, and Sean Dalton had gotten used to the quick payoff of the mining camps. He ran the ranch into the ground, left it to your granddaddy Kevin, and disappeared back up into the mountains, looking for another Sweet Mary. Your grandfather held on to the ranch, worked it up into quite a spread, and left it to your father, who unfortunately had more of Sean's blood in him than Kevin's."

"I don't need a history lesson." She cut him off and stood up abruptly. She didn't need Walker Evans to tell her about her own family, and she sure didn't need him to catalog her father's shortcomings.

"Well, you're going to get it, so sit back down . . . please."

The command didn't work, but the unexpected courtesy did. Blue perched herself on the edge of the couch, waiting for him to get to the end of his story and make whatever point he had in mind.

"In the forties Abel decided he'd had enough of mending fences. The Sweet Mary had brought the Daltons a fortune once. Why not twice? The claim was still in the family's name." Walker paused and set his mug on the end table, shifting his gaze away from her. "But your father, Blue, he wasn't quite the adventurer your great-grandfather was; he didn't want to go alone."

Blue felt her unease slacken and her confidence return. She had heard this story before, a couple of different versions from a couple of different men. She scooted deeper into the couch cushions and crossed her arms close to her chest and her legs one across the other. One booted foot swung in a tense rhythm. Walker Evans had run out of surprises.

"He took a partner, a legal partner with him into the—"

"Stop right there," she said. "If I believed every *partner* I've ever heard about, we'd have to pull up a chair to fit them all in the room."

"—mine," he continued, ignoring her interruption. "They found more than they'd bargained for, but the glory was short-lived. You see, Blue, they both wanted something else more than they wanted riches. The both wanted Lacey Ann Wilson."

Blue's foot froze in mid-swing, and her next breath lodged in her throat . . . *Lacey's Lode.*

"Whatever happened between the two men wasn't her fault. The only blameless one in the group was Lacey. She may not have chosen wisely, but she followed her heart and married the man she loved." His gaze strayed down to the floor, then back up again as he inhaled deeply and let the breath out slowly. "She married Jack, Blue. She married my father."

Storm clouds gathered in the dark eyes meeting his across the distance of the couch. He'd laid his claim, and she hadn't liked it. He'd expected no less than anger.

"So you're not a bastard after all," she conceded, her voice tight with the fury choking her throat.

"Not legally," he replied, ready to grab her if she decided to take off.

"Well, my father didn't mention your mother, your father, or *you* in his will, so shove that into your *legality*!" She rose to her feet, and Walker stood up with her.

"Your father was a coward, Blue. That's why he hid the damn stuff in the first place. He knew who it belonged to, and he knew he'd stolen Jack's share."

"So why didn't Jack do something about it?"

"Guilt," he said. He wasn't taking any chances with her. "He'd gotten the true prize, why they'd gone looking in the first place. Abel got mean after the two of them ran off. He threatened them both with revenge, called my father out and dared him to come and get his half. My mom got scared, so dad let it go. Forty years ago that wasn't such a loss, but times change, things become rarer . . . and prices rise, Blue. Do you know exactly what they found in the Sweet Mary?"

"Yes. Exactly."

"So do I. Have you checked with anybody about the value?"

"Without the pieces, he couldn't give me a price."

"But I bet he tried to follow you."

She nodded slowly, admitting to the first mistake she'd made when she'd started her quest. She'd approached the dealer with a story something along the lines of "a friend of mine," but soon realized she hadn't fooled him. She'd lost the man somewhere in New Mexico, and after that she'd kept her mouth shut.

"You need me," he said. "Not only for the directions but for protection."

"I can take care of myself. I've got Trapper, and if you'll give it back, I have my rifle." She wanted to call him a liar and be done with him but knew she couldn't. What he'd said explained too many things, filled in too many gaps, especially the bitterness her father had drawn around him like a cloak of shadow, a bitterness Blue swore had killed her mother before her time. She didn't accept Walker's story as a claim on her fortune, but she did accept it as truth. Lacey, and Lacey's Lode, didn't leave her much choice.

"Your dog is out of commission, and with me you won't need to use your rifle. I'll take care of any shooting that needs to be done."

Blue lowered her chin and rubbed her hand over her eyes, trying to think things through before she made another mistake. He'd bombarded her with too much information, and none of it what she'd wanted to hear. Lacey Evans, Walker's mother, the love of her father's life—it was all ancient history, and it was all too much.

Stupid girl. She'd thought her father's will was his final test for her, one last attempt from the grave to make her into the son he'd never had. Considering how he had treated her mother, she'd always thought he was damn lucky even to have gotten a daughter.

"Damn him," she murmured, squeezing her eyes tighter. She'd loved him despite his insensitive expectations, despite his drunken benders. She'd loved him, and he was still letting her down. The last thing he'd left her wasn't even his to give, not according to Walker Evans. *Damn him, too.*

A warm hand touched her shoulder. "Are you okay?"

Blue shrugged him off and turned her back on him, taking a couple of steps toward the fireplace. She dropped her hand to her side. "This is the deal. Take it or leave it. You give me the directions, and I'll give you the starting mark. Best man wins."

Her terminology brought a frown to Walker's face. The slender body and slight shoulders in front of him didn't belong to a man, and her confidence was way out of proportion with the facts. "I've already outtracked you once, Blue. What makes you think I can't do it twice?"

Nothing made her think he couldn't do it twice. She covered her face with her hand again and wrapped her other arm around her waist. She was slipping up, getting careless. She didn't know what to do anymore.

"Why don't we try my plan. Fifty-fifty. In a couple of days we can part company, both a little richer than when we met."

No. No. No. She hardened her resolve with each silent repetition. She hadn't come this far, she hadn't shot one man and outwitted four others to walk away with half. He'd been right last night. Lacey's Lode belonged to the person who found it; no other claim would stand up in court. She had to get there first and alone.

"Okay," she said, lifting her chin and staring at the clock on the fireplace mantel. A long sigh escaped her. "We'll do it your way. We'll start in the morning, early." It was ten o'clock. She had about eight hours before first light, eight hours to figure out a way to get the directions out of his head without him getting the mark out of hers.

Relief relaxed Walker's shoulders. He lifted his hand to the back of his neck and rubbed the tightness out of his muscles. "Good. We better hit the sack." The long hours of the day and the even longer hours of the night had worn him out, not physically but emotionally. Over the years he'd made a fine art out of avoiding just the kind of mess he'd been in since he'd taken off after her, or rather, since he'd caught her. Tracking her down hadn't sapped his strength nearly as much as dealing with her had.

"Fine." Blue looked around the cabin and saw her backpack where she'd dropped it by the door. She crossed the room and picked it up, then made a silent gesture for Trapper to follow. "We'll see you in the morning."

"Where do you think you're going?" he asked, instantly alert again.

"To get some sleep," she explained the obvious with a tired sigh, as if any fool could see what she was doing.

"You're not camping out tonight, and you're not sleeping in the barn."

"Well, I'm sure as hell not sleeping with you," she muttered, slipping the pack straps over her shoulders. Immediate realization of what she'd said stopped her with the pack only half on. She glanced up at him, hoping he hadn't heard, but one glance told her he'd heard plenty.

His easy grin barely held back the laughter she saw crinkling his eyes. "Nobody asked you to, Blue. You can have my bed. I've already moved into Janelle's old room."

"No thanks." She shrugged into the pack and wished the floor would open up and swallow her whole.

"I'm still not asking."

"You're telling me?" Her voice rose skeptically, along with both of her eyebrows. The man didn't know enough to quit while he was ahead.

"I'm offering you a bed and a hot bath. It's going to be a long day tomorrow. I want you rested."

She gave him a long-suffering glance. "I've never had anything but long days. One more isn't going to kill me."

Once again her statement told him more than he thought she wanted him to know. He'd had his share of long days, too, and they hadn't killed him either, but somehow he found himself wishing she hadn't had things as bad. He found himself wondering about the life that made her the woman she was—totally uncompromising, infinitely capable, knowledgeable about survival in the mountains, and incredibly naive about everything else.

"Take the bed and the bath, Blue. You look like you could use both. Tomorrow you can prove to me how tough you are."

Blue looked up, surprised by the gentleness in his voice. He wasn't laughing at her now. In fact, he almost sounded as if he cared. She hadn't had someone care about her since her father had died, not that he had really cared for her. But she couldn't deny the flicker of response she felt when Walker spoke so softly to her. The man had a way about him, a way of making her feel safe when she shouldn't, a way of making her say yes when she should say no.

With feigned nonchalance she let the pack slip back to the floor. "I need to take a walk, just be outside for a while. That jail cell was kind of . . . kind of . . ."

"I know. I'll wait up."

Confused as much by her feelings as his kindness, Blue nodded and let herself out the door, taking Trapper with her.

Walker listened to her cross the front porch, then the silence as she stepped onto the ground.

He had to force himself not to go after her, to make sure she found her way, to make sure she came back, and he knew the last reason had nothing to do with Dalton's Treasure or Lacey's Lode and everything to do with Blue. Damn. The lady kept sneaking up on him from the inside out. He didn't know how she did it, but she was better at it than he'd let anybody be for a long, long time.

He leaned back against the mantel and dragged his hand through his hair, and with each passing second he felt himself sinking in deeper over his head.

Blue finished toweling herself off, keeping one eye on the clean white shirt neatly folded on top of the clothes hamper. It had been under her towel and washcloth when she'd entered the bathroom, the position a sure sign of its purpose. He'd put it there for her to use. She didn't know what to do.

Wearing it didn't seem right. Not wearing it seemed rude, cowardly, and stupid to boot. Her own clothes were grimy with the dirt of three days on the trail and one in jail. She'd already used his shampoo, bathtub, and blow dryer, and had raided his medicine cabinet for a fresh bandage for her hand. If the truth be known, she'd used his razor too. The temptation had been too great, the results well worth her pang of guilt. She felt human again, and more than human she felt feminine—a rare, private luxury she seldom indulged in.

She reached out and ran a finger down the front of the shirt. The cloth was soft, cottony . . . tempting. Sighing, she looked at her clothes lying on the floor, and she knew she couldn't put them back on.

Walker leaned back in his chair, balancing it on two legs against the pine-paneled wall. He took another sip of coffee. What was she doing in there? Taking up residence? he wondered. He wouldn't have taken her for the bathroom-lounging type.

He should have let her sleep in the barn with her dog. Or more realistically, he should have slept in the barn. What did he think he was doing? Inviting her into his bed after what had happened last night. The longer she spent in there, the more time he had to think about it, the more time he had to remember, the more time he had to anticipate . . . nothing.

Nothing was going to happen. He could at least count on her for that. A short laugh escaped him, and he pushed off the chair and went back into the kitchen to warm his cup of coffee. He and Blue Dalton. He laughed softly again, ignoring the nervous edge in the sound. Even he had to have more sense than to tangle himself up with a she-cat.

Think of her as your kid sister, he told himself, and immediately another smile broadened his mouth in true humor. Janelle and Blue, now there was a mismatched pair if he'd ever seen one. Janelle never put anything on her body that didn't cost a hundred dollars, not anymore. Her days of ragged jeans were far behind her, and even before she'd married David, she'd never worn anything as ill-fitting as the pants Blue owned. She'd always known she was a woman, and Blue seemed never to have figured the fact out.

No, Blue didn't remind him of his kid sister, but if he tried, maybe he could convince himself she was off-limits anyway. Right, he thought, walk-

FREE – LIGHTED MAKEUP CASE!
FREE – 6 LOVESWEPT NOVELS!

- NO OBLIGATION
- NO PURCHASE NECESSARY

(DETACH AND MAIL CARD TODAY.)

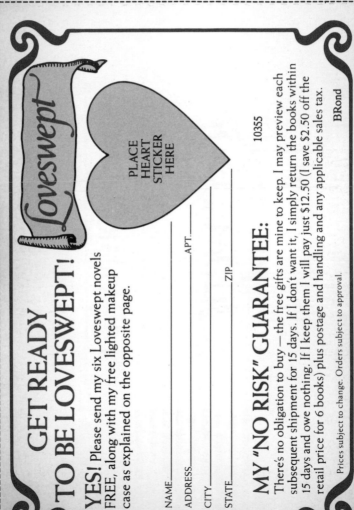

GET READY
TO BE LOVESWEPT!

YES! Please send my six Loveswept novels FREE, along with my free lighted makeup case as explained on the opposite page.

NAME _____

ADDRESS _____ APT. _____

CITY _____

STATE _____ ZIP _____

PLACE
HEART
STICKER
HERE

10355

MY "NO RISK" GUARANTEE:

There's no obligation to buy — the free gifts are mine to keep. I may preview each subsequent shipment for 15 days. If I don't want it, I simply return the books within 15 days and owe nothing. If I keep them I will pay just $12.50 (I save $2.50 off the retail price for 6 books) plus postage and handling and any applicable sales tax.

BRond

Prices subject to change. Orders subject to approval.

REMEMBER!

- The free books and gift are mine to keep!
- There is no obligation!
- I may preview each shipment for 15 days!
- I can cancel anytime!

(DETACH AND MAIL CARD TODAY.)

BUSINESS REPLY MAIL
FIRST-CLASS MAIL   PERMIT NO. 2456   HICKSVILLE, N.Y.

POSTAGE WILL BE PAID BY ADDRESSEE

Loveswept

Bantam Books
P.O. Box 985
Hicksville, NY 11802-9827

NO POSTAGE
NECESSARY
IF MAILED
IN THE
UNITED STATES

ing back into the living room, and maybe the sun wasn't going to come up in the morning.

Blue turned off the bathroom light and slipped out the door, meaning to make a quiet run to the bedroom. Walker's voice stopped her midway down the hall.

"I poured you a fresh cup of coffee."

She turned, clutching her dirty clothes in front of her. He was sitting at the kitchen table at the far end of the room, but the cabin wasn't big enough to make the distance a safe one, or to disguise the intrigued tilt of his head and the thoughtful expression on his face. His long johns shirt covered her to her knees and wrists, but under his watchful gaze, she felt exposed.

"Thanks, but I think I'll turn in." She made a small gesture with her hand.

"I've got hot chocolate. It might help you sleep."

Something had changed, and it took her a second to realize what it was; they were both in the same room and they weren't fighting. She found herself relaxing her guard, taking her cue from his friendly manner.

"That's okay. I don't think I'll have any trouble." She turned to go, then stopped and glanced back over her shoulder. For a moment she just looked at him, taking in the wild beauty of the man watching her. She held his gaze, feeling the pull of his thoughts in the shadowed depths of his eyes. He wanted her, and he was neither shy nor subtle about letting her know. The strength of his desire frightened her, but not nearly as much as the response she felt building inside herself.

Her gaze slipped from his, unable to cope with the silent communion flaring between them, but also unable to leave him completely. She visually traced the curve of his mouth, and the longing increased. She followed the line of his body across the breadth of his shoulders, and she remembered the dampness of tears. The power in the muscles apparent beneath the soft chamois of his shirt conjured up images of the night before when he'd held her in his arms.

But in the *ketoh* wrapped around his wrist she found the will to walk away. She knew what she had to do. She had to get to Lacey's Lode before he did.

"Good night, Walker," she whispered.

Watching her leave, Walker doubted her last words. The soft light in the hallway teased him with the shadowed movement of her body beneath his shirt. It mocked him by tracing the graceful strength of her legs and shining through the golden whiteness of her hair. Good night? He didn't think so. The only possible good night he could imagine entailed following her into his bedroom, wrapping her in his arms, kissing her until she melted from the heat, and then making love to her until the dawn of a very good morning.

Hell, he thought, pushing away from the table. He might as well start tossing and turning now. He'd had two restless nights on the trail trying to find her, and it had only gotten worse since he'd caught her. He'd never known a woman to cost him so much sleep.

Six

Walker awoke with a start, his first thought one of surprise that he'd slept at all; his second brought a jolt of adrenaline that had him scrambling out of bed and into his jeans. *Blue!* His feet hit the cold floor running. Lord knew what she was up to, or even if she'd stuck around.

Buttoning his pants, he raced across the hall and looked in her room. The bed was made, the blue and white quilt neatly tucked under the pillows, and neither she nor her dog were anywhere in sight. He swore under his breath and strode down the hall to the living room. Still no Blue.

You fool! You should have known better than to let her out of your sight for a second! She better have a helluva start, because when he caught up with her, he was going to . . . going to . . .

The sound of laughter outside stopped him in his tracks. He walked over to the window, lifted an edge of curtain, and along with relief, felt all the problems he'd had in the night come back in full force.

She was kneeling in the soft green meadow grass, talking to her dog and tossing bits of bread to the gray jays daring enough to get close. Pale sunshine haloed the golden strands of her hair and illuminated the delicate profile of her face, revealing a carefree, angelic countenance. Walker stood perfectly still, mesmerized by the early-morning scene and the slight woman filling it with beauty and light. She laughed again and tucked her hair behind her ear, revealing the sweet curves of a smile he felt all the way to his gut. He'd never seen her happy before, never seen her smile, and the effect was nothing short of totally wondrous and totally demoralizing.

He dropped the curtain and cussed softly all the way into the bathroom. Even after the whole thing was over, she still wouldn't have any reason to smile at him. He'd tied her up, attempted to seduce her, bullied her, and trapped her by burning the map. Guilt and women were a rare mixture in his life, but without any effort on her part Blue Dalton was heaping a load of it on his head.

Blue finished feeding the jays, not having to work very hard to entice the biggest one with her last piece of toast. Not even Trapper's nearness dissuaded the camp robber from his free meal. The bird landed with a screech, then hopped closer, snatched the bread off the ground, and flew off in a flurry of wings.

"Funny bird." She laughed, absently stroking Trapper's soft coat. A morning breeze cooled her cheeks, and she lifted her face into the rising sun. The day was coming, and after a long night with her topographical maps and her compass, she was ready to face it. Her plan required skill, concentration, and an artless flair for deception. In other words, she had to lie through her teeth and do it with conviction. Nothing less would fool Walker Evans. By nightfall she'd have the directions inside his head, and he'd have nothing.

Her smile faded at the thought. She mentally shrugged off the pang of guilt. What was Walker Evans to her except another in a long line of men who'd tried to take her inheritance? If the father hadn't had enough guts to go after what was his, what did it matter how much courage the son had? She was the one who'd figured everything out. He hadn't been there when she'd sunk herself deep into Lake Agnes, and he hadn't been there when O'Keefe had cornered her in the cabin, a fact much to O'Keefe's advantage. Walker had made his views about forcing women against their will very plain, in words and in deed.

Unconsciously she touched her fingers to her lips and once again felt the warmth of his mouth on hers. She closed her eyes and dropped her hand back into her lap. No one else had ever made her feel what she'd felt when he'd kissed her. No one else had ever touched her with such tenderness and passion. She didn't believe it now, had barely believed it even as his slow, sensual explorations of her mouth had taught her everything a kiss could be. He'd held her so closely, his strong arms around her, his hand on her face, guiding her deeper into the mystery of the gentle, consuming strokes of his tongue down the length of hers.

She opened her eyes, suddenly shivering in the cool air, and looked back at the cabin, wondering if he had awakened. He'd been sleeping restlessly when she'd left. She hadn't meant to look at him, but his door had been open, and she'd been disturbingly, undeniably curious. He slept on his stomach, and he didn't wear pajamas. More useless information, she'd told herself, but she'd stood there anyway, watching dawn trace shadows across the muscles in his back, watching the darkness of his skin turn the color of coffee with cream in the increasing light. And for a fleeting moment, before she'd turned away, she'd imagined herself lying there with him, warm and safe in his embrace, waking him with a kiss.

She shook her head in annoyance as the image returned and rose to her feet. "Come on, Trapper. I'll get your breakfast."

Walker had done another nice thing last night besides get her out of jail. He'd taken her stuff out of her Jeep and put it all in the bed of his truck. This morning she'd dug some clean but wrinkled clothes out of her suitcase and changed in the bathroom, that time avoiding his room. Now she went back to the truck for Trapper's food and bowls.

Walker saw her come around the side of the cabin. He leaned across the kitchen sink and knocked the quarter-paned window open with a light bang of his fist. "How do you like your eggs?"

"Cooked. Really cooked," she said, looking up at him from where she crouched by the water spigot.

From that particular angle, and without any forethought on his part, he could see down the front of her chambray shirt. If the woman had been inclined to wear clothes that fit instead of everything big and baggy, the angle wouldn't have made a difference. But she wasn't, and the angle did. The gentle rises of her breasts were exposed just enough to give his heart a start.

"Cooked. Right," he mumbled, ducking his head back inside. When he was sure she couldn't see him, he gave in to the smile tugging at his mouth. He'd been tempted by the best, by women who'd made vocations out of teasing, women who'd made no secret of what they'd wanted from him. But Blue, like every other feeling she aroused in him— and aroused was the operative word—tempted him without even knowing it.

"Cooked like your goose, Walker," he whispered to himself, cracking eggs into the frying pan.

Blue finished setting up Trapper's food and water and checked his stitches before heading inside the cabin. On the porch step she took one last look at the morning light spilling over the high ridges of the Rawahs. The peaks glistened with remnants of winter's snow. She took a deep breath, loving the dew-fresh air, the abundance of wilderness spreading out around her, and the comforting knowledge she was finally back where she belonged.

"Breakfast's ready, Blue. Come and get it," she heard him holler from the kitchen. His words brought the faintest smile to her lips. He made it sound as if he'd been cooking her breakfast for years.

Her smile quickly faded. She had to lie to him. To trust him was a sucker's bet. Just because he'd kissed her didn't make him a better man than all the rest, no matter who his mother had or had not loved. Straightening her shoulders, Blue strode into the cabin, determined to play her plan out to the last detail.

Warmth from last night's fire remained in the simply furnished living room, washing over her chilled skin with a gentle touch. She shrugged out of her jacket and hung it by the door. In daylight the cabin seemed as fresh and welcoming as the mountains outside. Sunlight streamed through the thick-glassed windows and burnished the pine paneling to a golden glow. Things she hadn't noticed before struck her one by one: the casual disarray of books on the shelves in the corner, many of them open or marked with a slip of paper; the hutch next to the dining room table, filled with mismatched china; the sun-catcher in the window shaped like a trout, casting rainbows against the walls.

Whatever else he was, Walker Evans was no drifter. The cabin was a home not a stopping place. It made facing him that much more difficult when she passed through the entry into the kitchen.

Walker sensed her presence before he heard or saw her. He purposely kept his attention on the eggs. "Plates are in the cupboard next to the sink. Coffee mugs are hanging on the wall. Help yourself."

Blue did, then on impulse warmed his cup with coffee from the pot. In the small kitchen she had to reach around him, and as soon as she did she realized something besides impulse had prompted the gesture. She'd wanted to get closer to him, had been irresistibly drawn by his nearness and her memories of sunlight on his skin.

Walker felt her brush against his arm. He looked down at the flaxen head below his shoulder and half-turned toward her. "Thanks."

"You're welcome." Flustered, she set the pot on the stove and started to back away, but he reached out and captured her wrist. A shallow breath escaped her. She didn't dare to raise her eyes. The bracelet glinted up at her, banding his dark skin and the light-brown hair dusting his forearm. The sleek silver contrasted with the prominent veins running down the back of his hand, its beauty matching the strength she felt in his grasp.

"You should have let me fix this," he said, lifting her hand into the light and tracing the new bandage with his thumb.

"They looked at it in Walden, put some stuff on it, and I cleaned it again and rebandaged it last night." Her gaze slipped down to the waistband of his jeans, and heat rose in her cheeks. The denim was soft, worn to the contours of his hips and the junctures of his thighs, the creases indelibly marked by faded color. He'd pulled her into his lap two nights ago and she'd felt him against her.

"Is your tetanus up-to-date?"

"Yes." She gave a little shrug. "Seems I'm always doing something to myself."

"Now, why do I find that so easy to believe?" His soft laughter washed over her, heightening her blush. He released her and returned his attention to finishing their breakfast.

It took Blue a second or two to remember what she'd been doing. Then with a jerky movement she opened the cupboard to get their plates, determined to put a tight rein on her overheated imagination. He'd touched her, and parts of her had crumbled inside—the smart parts. She wouldn't let it happen again.

He filled the plates as she held them out. "I put some things on the table I thought you might be interested in."

Still disconcerted by her thoughts, she didn't respond.

"Did your father ever tell you where Lacey's Lode came from?" he asked.

"No. He barely talked about it at all . . . except when he was drinking."

He didn't comment on her admission. "Well, neither of them could ever be positive, but my dad had plenty of theories, most of which he pursued with a diligence I wish he'd used on finding the jewelry instead. I guess your old man had him too scared to do that, though."

"He wasn't a scary man," she came to her father's defense. "He was quiet, kept his own counsel, but he never hurt anybody."

"You come by it honestly then." He set the pan back on the stove, and when she looked up at him with a quizzical glance, he explained further. "You're the quietest damn woman I ever met. Half the time I can read your mind, and the other half I don't have a clue. Do you ever tell anybody what's going on in your head?"

Read her mind? She sincerely hoped not, for she knew beyond a shadow of a doubt which of her thoughts she hadn't been able to conceal. Her thoughts of him came upon her too suddenly, with too much force, to hide. "No one has ever asked," she stated bluntly, and started to head for the table in the living room.

But he didn't let her go, stopping her with a question. "And if someone did? If I did? Would you tell me?"

"No." She didn't need to think about her answer. He was the last person on earth she'd tell her thoughts to, since lately most of them centered around deceiving him and more than a few of them dwelled on kissing him again.

Walker followed her to the table, carrying their coffee cups, no less mystified by the lady than he'd been before.

"Have you ever heard the term 'old pawn'?" he asked, turning the conversation to something he did understand and knew would interest her. He sat down and opened one of the books on the table.

"I saw it once. Used it once."

"To the man you asked about the value of the pieces." It was a statement of fact not a question, and Blue wondered again about him reading her mind. "I bet he didn't believe you at first."

"Not at first," she admitted.

"Read this." He turned the book toward her.

Blue skimmed the first couple of paragraphs, until her attention was caught by a date and the word "robbery." She lowered her fork to her plate and pulled the book closer, and the further she read, the more fascinated she became. *The B & E Trading Post . . . 1898 . . . armed outlaws . . . Slater Gang tracked into the southern ranges of the Colorado Rockies.* She flipped the page. *Buckner killed in pursuit . . . Edward sold post to Wattel brothers in spring of 1990.*

"Doesn't say what they got away with," she said.

"Doesn't have to. It was a trading post in New Mexico, close to the Indian reservations. They all had pawn vaults, and in every pawn vault was a treasure hoard of Indian jewelry. Whatever else they took, they wouldn't have left the silver and turquoise."

"This isn't proof," she insisted, not wanting to believe yet another story of theft related to her inheritance.

"The only proof we'll ever have is if the pawn tickets are still attached to the jewelry when we find it."

"Then what?" She glanced up from the book.

"Then we can name our price."

"What about descendants?"

"Whose? Buckner's? Edward probably wrote the loss off when he sold the business. The Wattel brothers started with a clean slate. The Indians got their value when they pawned their hard goods, and Slater stole the stuff. Evans and Dalton, Blue, those are the only descendants we need to worry about, unless you want to spend another hundred years sorting everything out."

He watched her slip back into the quiet deepness of her thoughts, her delicate jaw set as she cut off a piece of egg. He wondered what else he could do to draw her out. The conversation obviously hadn't worked. Staring at her probably didn't help either.

But damn she was pretty. A rainbow from the window caught in her hair, slipping to grace the tawny skin of her cheek every time she moved her head. He had the wildest compulsion to capture it with his thumb in a caress. He wished she would smile again. He wished she would look up at him with her dark-brown eyes and smile at him.

Ha, he thought with a self-derisive grin. This was the day they'd find what they'd both been looking for, and then she'd go on her way. He was tempted to lie to her just to keep her around a while longer, but that wouldn't be right. If nothing else, he wanted her to know him as a man of his word, the one man who hadn't tried to cheat her.

"Looks like a good day today." He offered up the weather, the most innocuous thing he could think to talk about.

Blue cast a glance out the far window, avoiding even the slightest chance of accidentally running into his green-flecked, amber eyes, then looked back to her plate. "Yes."

The rainbow on her skin refracted with her movement, tangling in her hair and reappearing as a palette brush of color below her cheekbone. Walker forced his gaze away from her, before he actually did reach out and touch her.

They finished eating in silence, Blue staring at her plate, and Walker trying not to stare at her. When he'd downed his last piece of toast, he stood up and walked over to the bookcase on the other side of the living room. He came back with a roll of maps and set them on the table.

"Time to get to work," he said, flattening out the maps. "Show me the mark."

Blue fumbled with her napkin, not daring to

give in too easily, not exactly sure how to lie with conviction. With all the thieving and lying already attributed to Lacy's Lode, she didn't know why hers had to feel like the worst. "You'll have to give me something first," she said, buying a moment's time.

He glanced at her. "I already gave you my word. Isn't that enough?"

"No."

Fine, he thought. If he'd been in her position, he wouldn't have given anything away for free either.

"Two hundred twenty degrees," he said, conceding the first of his carefully memorized directions.

"How far?"

"Two."

"Two what?"

"He didn't say, but it's got to be miles. He gets more detailed later."

"How detailed?"

"Paces, different bearings, maybe landmarks."

Good, Blue thought, rising from her chair and joining him at the side of the table. She could count paces and make compass bearings when they were on the trail.

Resting one hand on her hip, she looked down at the map of North Park and made a mental note of two miles on a 220-degree bearing from the true mark, knowing she'd have to map it out later for accuracy. Then she placed the tip of her finger a fraction of an inch, more than a mile, to the left.

Walker grinned. She'd landed right where he'd expected, smack dab on the North Star ranch.

"The starting point is about here. Do you have a bigger-scale map of this area?" she asked.

"How does five inches to the mile sound?"

"Like you made it yourself," she answered warily, slanting him a glance.

"Almost. I enlarged the U.S. topo." He pulled another map out of the pile and set it on top. Blue took one look and immediately went on alert. He'd done more than enlarge the map; he'd filled in all the details: the ranch house, the outbuildings, the fence lines. The North Star was spread out before her in all its dilapidated glory. Some of the areas were shaded in, others had notations written on them, all of the additions bespeaking of a search as thorough as her own.

"You've been doing your homework," she said, using the flip remark to hide her agitation. "I should have you arrested for trespassing."

"I could return the favor," he countered calmly.

Blue bit back an angry retort, and said only, "Let's get going and get this over with."

She left him standing at the table and strode over to the door. Walker watched her slip into her jacket and grab her pack before she disappeared out the door. For a person on the verge of finding a fortune, even half a fortune, she didn't seem very excited. But then, his own excitement about Lacey's Lode seemed strangely subdued this morning.

Maybe he'd looked too long without success to believe it would come today. Maybe he'd hung too many expectations on old dreams. Or maybe something more important had just walked out of his cabin.

·   ·   ·

"This is too easy," Walker muttered, pacing the length of the North Star ranch-house porch.

Blue silently agreed, cursing herself for not thinking faster when they'd pulled up. All she'd been thinking of was getting him as far away as possible from the true starting mark, and of giving herself an easily identifiable point to work from later when she remapped the directions in the privacy of his bedroom.

But the ranch house? She could have done better blindfolded if he hadn't laid his hand on her shoulder when she'd leaned over the bed of the truck to retrieve her pack. The gesture had been casual; her reaction had been anything but casual. He'd lifted her pack out for her, then grinned at her obvious discomfort, and, she was sure, the blush she'd felt stealing up her cheeks.

"Well, this is it." She knelt on the porch and pulled a compass out of her backpack. "Two-twenty?" she asked, as if she'd forget a number she'd burned into her memory.

"Yeah," he answered, coming over and kneeling beside her. He unrolled the map, anchoring the curled corners with his knees and his large hands, bringing his body much too close to suit her.

She straightened up.

"Relax, Blue. I don't bite," he drawled.

Liar, she thought. He'd bit her, quite gently, on the neck two nights ago. Exasperated with herself and the wayward course of her mind, she tucked her hair behind her ear and forced her concentration on the business at hand. When she had the bearing, he measured off the miles and made a mark.

His eyes immediately narrowed, and Blue cussed

silently again. From the looks of the map, she had them hanging off a cliff. The contour intervals were damn close together, but neither of them mentioned the fact.

"Let's go," was all he said, rising with the map in his hands. With a few, quick moves he had it rolled up and stuffed into his back pocket.

Blue hefted her pack to her back, knowing she wasn't going to get anything else out of him until they'd followed this wild-goose chase to the end.

Seven

By the middle of the third day Blue was beginning to doubt if they'd ever get to the end of anything. She had rimrocked them straight out from the North Star, and they'd spent hours backtracking and bushwhacking their way to the bottom of the cliff by another trail. Abel's convoluted directions had effectively ruined the rest of that first afternoon and the next, and had pretty much turned the current one into a swamp of frayed tempers, muttered curses, and circular paths.

Groaning softly, she unloaded her pack and dropped to her knees. Let Walker wear a hole in the forest floor; she was taking a break. She dug an orange out of a side pocket and arranged her pack and then herself against a tree trunk. She wasn't worried about losing him; he'd been crashing around the same quadrant for an hour, and she knew he was never going to find what he was looking for, the "BRK" from the map he'd burned. Bear Rock, she'd told him. He'd believed her, and now she was just waiting for him to find some rock that from some angle looked something like a bear. Then she'd get the fifth in the long line of directions her father had left. She'd never known her father as a puzzle lover, but he'd sure put his all into this game of hide-and-seek; much as Walker was. But the man had to give up sooner or later, and she'd never give up. She'd have Lacey's Lode by the end of the week.

"Or die trying," she muttered, digging her fingers into the peel and tearing it away piece by piece. She'd give him one more day, and if they hadn't killed each other by then, she was going to shoot him. The thought alone made her feel better, as if she were back in control of at least one part of her life. She bit into the orange and ended up nipping the tip of her tongue. She quickly pressed it against her teeth and sucked hard.

"Damn him," she mumbled around the fruit, blaming Walker for her clumsiness. The man grated on her nerves, set her teeth on edge. She couldn't get within ten feet of him without wanting to run the other way, and the biggest room in his cabin barely measured fifteen feet in length. They were like two caged cats at night, in much too small a cage. Hell, even the western slope of the Medicine Bows wasn't big enough for the both of them. Her only consolation was that he didn't seem any more pleased with the situation than she was, or so she told herself every evening when he muttered his gruff good night.

He was ready to break; she could feel it. His attempts at conversation had become rarer, his smiles even more so. Two days of her company had stretched his patience thinner than thin. She could have told him she was no peach to live with when he'd come up with his stupid plan, and saved them both a lot of trouble. She'd heard the opinion expressed too many times in Galveston not to have believed it to be the truth.

Men, who could understand them? She let out a soft sound of disgust. One lousy kiss, you'd think she could forget one lousy kiss. One kiss she found playing over and over in her mind. She'd awakened about three A.M. with an incredible set of images crowding her subconscious. They had made facing him this morning more embarrassing than usual. She'd kept wondering if the muscles in his chest and arms really bunched and moved under his skin as gracefully as she'd dreamed, or if his skin really tasted musky-sweet, or if it was truly possible for him to move over and cover her body in such a way that she melted inside.

She'd had a terrible time getting back to sleep, and only a couple of hard trail hours had been able to banish the last shreds of her oversensitive awareness of him. In truth, she realized the grueling pace they were keeping during the days was probably the only thing keeping her on an even keel at night.

But the pace was taking its toll in other areas.

She slipped lower on her pack, arranging her bottom in the bed of pine needles below the tree, grateful for the moment of rest.

Walker had reached the end of his rope, and finding her all stretched out and comfortable didn't improve his mood. He swept his hat off his head and used his forearm to wipe away the sweat, and he kept staring at Blue. He was beginning to smell a rat, and the rat looked as though she didn't have a care in the world, let alone a treasure to find. All the time he'd been pushing his nobler instincts to the limit, she'd been lying to him. None of his directions made a damn bit of sense on the trail they were following. Landmarks weren't where they were supposed to be. Paces dead-ended into granite walls. Hell, they'd even gotten rimrocked the first day out. At the time, he'd given old Abel more credit than he deserved for being one tough bastard to follow. Days later he knew Abel's daughter had lied to him about the starting mark.

Damn! He hadn't so much as accidentally touched her since their first night together; he'd been careful not to. He'd figured they had a deal, and he hadn't wanted to complicate it with anything else. She'd obviously decided to complicate things plenty by lying. He'd put up with her moody silences, her reclusive manner, and the way she disappeared into her room every time he got within arm's length of her. And what had it gotten him? Nothing. Not one unguarded word, not one kind glance, not one single smile. He didn't even want to think about all the other things it hadn't gotten him— such as closer to her.

Well, the lady was about to learn a few things about him. One, he wasn't going to let her get away with her scheming tricks; and two, with a minimum of effort, he could be damn hard, if not impossible, to ignore. He rested his shoulder against a pine, his mouth a grim line. He'd been handling her with kid gloves, but she didn't need to be handled with kid gloves; she needed an iron hand. Rules didn't matter; she didn't recognize any rules. She'd dragged him around the mountain for the last time.

Pushing off the tree, he slapped his hat on his thigh, raising some dust, and began walking toward her.

Despite his quiet tread, Blue heard him coming. She cocked her hat on the back of her head and glanced up. "Did you find it?"

"No."

The tiredness she heard in his voice made hiding her smug smile a prudent move. The way he sat down next to her, facing her and so close their hips touched, wiped any thoughts of smiling right out of her mind.

"Orange?" she asked after clearing a nervous tremor from her throat.

"Thanks." He dropped his hat on the ground and shrugged out of his pack, and Blue found herself momentarily mesmerized by the sight of muscle moving beneath cloth, supple and hard, stretching his shirt sleeves when he flexed. Her gaze slid down the length of his arm, following the movement to his hands. They were workingman's hands, weathered by the sun and the cold, chiseled to a rough perfection by the elements and the strength with which they were used. He took the orange and tore the remaining segments in half, giving her a share.

"You know, Blue, I'm beginning to think we're going about this all wrong." He bit down on the whole half of the orange, exposing straight, white teeth. With the back of his hand he wiped the juice off his mouth. Sunlight added golden highlights to the tawny mane of his hair, reminding her for a moment of how the silky strands had felt running through her fingers.

"Wrong?" she asked, her mouth suddenly dry.

"Yeah. We're losing too much time running back and forth between my place and the North Star. I think it's time we got serious. Tomorrow when we come, we're coming to stay. I've got a two-man tent, so you don't have to worry about living out of a lean-to. We'll set up camp"—he looked around the area and shrugged—"here, I guess. We can't be that far from Lacey's Lode. There's only one direction after Bear Rock, which I'll be damned if I can find." He took another big bite out of the orange, ignoring the neat segments Mother Nature had put there for easy consumption.

Of course he couldn't find it, she thought. It didn't exist. But that was the least of her problems. Two-man tent? Not even a four-man tent would be big enough to hold the two of them, not to her satisfaction.

"I don't think . . . uh . . . why don't I try to find it," she finished after a false start, pushing herself to her feet. There had to be a rock out there somewhere that she could convince him looked like a bear. Then he'd give her the last direction. Two-man tent? Not if she could help it.

"Sure, Blue," he drawled, taking her place by the tree. "Give it your best shot." He lifted his hat off the ground and settled it over his face as he made himself comfortable. "Let me know if you find anything."

Blue brushed the pine needles off her backside, watching him settle in. She'd find a bear-shaped rock if she had to chisel one out herself.

Walker heard her stride off into the forest, and beneath his hat he grinned.

Blue pounded another tent stake into the ground, swearing with each clink of the flat end of the ax on metal. "Bear Rock," she muttered to Trapper under her breath. There was no Bear Rock. Didn't the man know when to give up? He should have just given her the last direction last night as she'd suggested, supposedly so they could double-check everything they'd done up to this point and find out where they were going and where they'd gone wrong. Or rather, where he'd gone wrong. She had *her* ducks in a row, she thought in irritation, conveniently forgetting she was the one who had set him up to fail.

"Looks good, Blue, and in record time," he said, coming up behind her with another load of firewood. "I could use you on my hunting trips. Most of the men I guide can't tell a tent pole from their rifles. If this doesn't pan out and you need a job, I'll hire you next fall."

Blue gave the stake another good whack, and, maintaining her silence, shook the rain fly out over the tent. Trapper shied away at the flapping material and wandered a little way off. Traitor, she thought.

"Last year was the wildest ever," he continued, dropping the wood next to the fire ring and lifting his hat to push back his hair. "There was a man over by Grand Lake. He shot a mule, thinking it was a bear, and all he had was a deer license." His low chuckle rolled over her as he settled his hat back on his head.

Blue knelt and began tying down the fly. "Everybody knows you should mark your domestic animals during hunting season," she said, jerking the rope.

Walker knelt beside her, tying the next string on the fly. "The mule was marked all right. Had a couple of fluorescent streamers hanging from his halter."

Blue shot him a disbelieving glance, for once unaware of his closeness. "The man shot an animal in halter?"

"Three times. Split his ear open, got him across the withers, and finally felled him by hitting him in the knee."

"My God!" she whispered, her eyes widening. "Don't tell me he stopped there!"

"Apparently he was pretty shook up, what with almost getting attacked by a *bear*"—his tone added a wry twist to the word—"but someone else had the sense to put the animal out of its misery."

"Someone should have put the hunter out of his misery. Good Lord! The people they let loose with guns in these hills." She finished her first knot, shaking her head, and moved to work on the third.

Walker skirted by her and started on the fourth, a broad grin curving his mouth. "Yeah. I've run into some pretty unpredictable ones myself lately."

"Really?" she asked, then saw his smile. Recovering quickly, she slipknotted the fly string onto the guideline and said, "I've run into a couple lately myself."

Walker laughed. "I guess between the two of us we ought to be able to handle whatever comes along from here on out."

The barest smile teased her mouth. "Yeah," she said. "I guess so."

Her smile warmed him in that strange way of hers—from the inside out—and for a long moment he wished she was there beside him by choice, setting up camp in the early-morning light.

"Can you smell it?" Walker asked hours later, stopping in a glade of budding aspens. A graying sky cast shadows through the slender white tree trunks, dappling the spring grass into muted verdant hues. They were about three fourths of the way through a half-mile semicircle he'd mapped out for their meaningless search for Bear Rock.

"Rain," she answered, weariness evident in the softness of her voice and her bent-over stance in the meadow. Her hands rested on her thighs as she looked upward through the trees.

"Or snow." He glanced up at the sky and the low bank of clouds rolling in over the mountains. He'd been keeping a relentless pace, hoping she'd give up and confess, or slip up and reveal her lie. He'd have tried intimidation if he'd thought it would work, but every time he'd pushed her, she'd pushed harder, and he'd ended up watching his back. He'd kept her rifle, but she had her dog, and though he and the animal had reached a compromise of sorts, he didn't doubt whose side Trapper would be on if voices were raised in anger.

"Or snow," she agreed, feeling the bite in the air. "Maybe we should break camp and head home." With effort she managed to keep her voice steady and her legs from trembling. They'd left the cabin at the crack of dawn and hadn't stopped since. For the first time she realized she'd been lucky to have kept ahead of him for even one day when he'd been tracking her across North Park. The man had been named perfectly—Walker. Nonstop Walker. Pick-'em-up-and-put-'em-down Walker. Wear-her-into-the-ground Walker. The previous day's tiredness was a burst of energy compared to this day's bone-aching exhaustion.

"You afraid of the snow, Blue?" he asked, giving her a quizzical look.

"Of course not." She drew on her reserves for an unladylike snort and hefted the day pack higher on her shoulders. She didn't care if he walked to hell and back; she'd be right there behind him. And when he finally gave up, she'd go find what was hers. She was so close, one map mark away.

"Then we'll keep going. When we finish this area, we'll start again to the northwest. By nightfall we'll be sitting on Bear Rock."

By nightfall Blue doubted if she could sit on her own behind and stay upright. They dragged into camp, a camp covered with three inches of snow. The whole scene was too much to bear with her usual fortitude. She took one look at the cold snow falling through the trees, the cold fire ring, the cold tent, and decided her best bet was the latter. Deep inside her down sleeping bag was her only chance for what she needed most—to drop like a stone and not get up again until morning, if then.

Walker shrugged out of his pack and deposited it in the clear spot beneath the tent fly, all the while watching her carefully for signs of collapse.

He'd pushed her too hard, up one hill and down the next, trying to prove—what? He didn't know anymore. He gave his head a quick shake of disgust. Her gloves were brown cotton working gloves; the fingers were cut off halfway down, and she kept curling her hands into fists to keep them warm. Her baggy jeans were staying on her hips by the grace of a miracle. Her Stetson was pulled so low on her head, he couldn't even begin to see her eyes. The dropping temperature reddened her thin, tanned cheeks and the tip of her nose to the color of the bandana tied around her neck.

He felt like the world's biggest bastard standing there, watching her fight the exhaustion bowing her head. He wanted to gather her up and share the warmth and energy he still had in abundance. Instead, he walked quietly behind her and slipped the pack from her shoulders, making sure he had one hand ready in case she crumpled.

She groaned softly, and he caught her around the waist and held her until she could find her new center of balance.

Blue rested against him, letting her eyes drift closed and wishing she never had to move again. Every part of her hurt. The strength of his hard body supported her in a way she found difficult to resist. To lean back against him and fall asleep on her feet seemed an even better option than crawling into the cold tent alone; he, at least, was warm.

Don't be ridiculous, she told herself, drawing her strength up from way down deep inside and pushing away from him.

"Thanks," she murmured, feeling foolish for needing him for even a moment.

"Anytime," he said, with a strange edge of harshness in his voice. "Why don't you get inside and get comfortable. I'll bring you something to eat."

He'd have to, she thought. If dinner had been up to her, they both would have gone hungry. She dropped to her knees on her pack and unzipped the tent, then rolled over and sat down inside, making sure her boots didn't dirty the interior. When they were unlaced, she took them off and hit them together to knock away the snow.

Walker didn't miss a single, agonizingly slow movement she made. He heard her whisper a stream of soft curses as she eased down on the sleeping bags, leaving only her two white-socked feet hanging outside. After a second she pulled them inside, groaning under her breath.

"I think she'll live, boy," he said to the shepherd, reaching down and scratching the dog behind the ears.

Blue lay quietly, listening to him rustle around the camp starting a fire and making dinner. She couldn't take much more. She'd finally met her match. This morning when she'd unrolled their sleeping bags, her biggest problem had been sharing the tent with him. In truth, before lunch she'd spent more time fretting about the close quarters awaiting her than she had worrying over Lacey's Lode. By late afternoon her priorities had begun to shift to the muscles in her legs and the ache in her back. About five o'clock she'd realized she'd never outlast him. The man wasn't going to give up, not in her lifetime. Her choices had dwindled to telling him the truth or walking away with nothing. The second choice was ruinous. The first was downright dangerous.

She didn't think he'd physically hurt her. If nothing else, she did know that about him. But, oh, brother, would he be mad, really mad.

Wincing, she rolled onto her side and wrapped her arms around her waist, trying to still her shivering and conserve her body warmth. They'd argued plenty, but she'd only seen him angry once, the night she'd called him pretty boy, the night he'd stopped her heart with a single furious glare. She preferred not to dwell upon the night he'd stopped her heart with a single incredible kiss.

No, she thought, stifling a yawn. She didn't want to think about kissing, not when she was cold and hungry and so tired, even breathing took effort—and certainly not when she was curled up inside half of a two-man tent, of which the other half belonged to him.

But as happened every evening when sleep pulled at the fabric of her defenses and her mind drifted off toward never-never land, his kiss was the image she held on to—his mouth, hard and soft at the same time, opening over hers, teasing her, her own response welling up inside.

Walker knelt between the tent flaps, watching her sigh softly in her sleep, her mouth parting in unintentional invitation, and he wished he'd taken her home, where he wouldn't be subjected to her special brand of torture. Lantern light caught the flaxen strands of hair feathering over her ear. The soft glow turned her skin into golden cream and her mouth into pure temptation.

Innocence incarnate, he thought, knowing she'd done nothing to instigate the sharp ache he suddenly felt. She'd done nothing but react to the pressure he'd put on her since he'd tracked her down and carried her home. She'd done nothing but be the woman she was, not physically strong enough to tangle with him by his very physical rules, and not helpless enough to give up.

"Blue," he said softly, setting aside the thermos and the pan of stew. "Wake up." He reached out and laid his hand on her arm, resisting the urge to stroke her cheek and tuck her hair behind her ear, resisting the desire to caress her face, to feel her satin skin beneath his rough fingers.

"No," she murmured, more a sigh than a word. The uncharacteristic petulance in the sound brought a grin to his face. *No.* It was the most vulnerable thing she'd ever said to him. The first chink she'd revealed in her armor of self-sufficiency.

"Come on, Blue." His hand slid down to her hip, shaking her a little. "You can't sleep until you've eaten."

"I'm already asleep," she told him on a whisper, dreamily aware of the weight and warmth of his large hand touching her.

Walker moved farther into the tent and stretched out beside her, leaning on his elbow and resting his head in his hand. For a long time he lay there next to her, watching her chest rise and fall with her soft breaths, following the play of shadows across her face. He would have continued the pleasurable if dangerous pastime if she hadn't shivered, reminding him of what he'd come for. "Come on, Blue. You're not asleep yet, and you're not going to want to miss what I've cooked up."

"Hmm?"

"Antelope stew and socks."

"Socks?" Her eyes opened slowly, barely focused, and Walker felt as if he could drown in those midnight depths of darkest brown. "Why did you cook the socks?"

"To keep your feet warm." Unable to resist any longer, he reached out and slowly brushed his thumb up the delicate arch of her cheek. Thick sable lashes fluttered closed again as she sighed, and he lowered his head close to her ear, needing to touch her with his mouth. A length of tawny hair fell over his shoulder, blocking them from the light, but he didn't need light to taste, to feel, to remember the curves of her face. His arm automatically slid around her waist. "And I brought hot chocolate," he murmured, teasing her skin with his lips.

"Sounds . . . good." Her breath caught at the gentle forays of his mouth, at the sheer power of his body leaning over her, and she felt herself waking up in startling, increasing degrees, which did nothing to ease the lethargy in her limbs. "Walker?"

"Yeah?" he asked softly, nuzzling her neck.

"I didn't"—her eyes opened on a gasp as he pulled her bandana down and found a particularly sensitive spot near her nape—"I didn't . . . think we were going to do this again."

"We were wrong," he said, his voice rough.

"But—"

"But you're cold and you need to eat," he finished her sentence, stopping himself before she had the chance to tell him no. The lady needed to learn how to say yes. He kissed her quickly on the mouth before rolling to a sitting position. "I hope you don't mind sharing the pan. I didn't want to dirty a bunch of dishes."

"No, I . . . uh . . . don't mind." She pushed herself up and tried not to be so damn confused, but creating confusion seemed to be his forte when it came to her. For two enemies, they acted more like friends, and sometimes he treated her like more than even a friend.

"You go ahead and start." He handed her the stew pan. "Let me see your feet."

Wrapping her gloved hands around the pan for warmth, she did as he asked and lifted one foot.

"Eat," he commanded, peeling away her cold socks. He reached for her other foot and did the same. From beneath his shirt he pulled out a warm, almost hot, pair of clean, dry socks and rolled them onto her feet.

"Lordy." She sighed, her eyes closing. "That feels like heaven."

No it didn't, he silently disagreed. The socks felt warm; kissing her felt like heaven. He'd done some pretty stupid things in his life, but falling for Blue Dalton had to rank right up there with the worst of them—or the best of them. He didn't know anymore, but he knew he was falling for her, and he was falling hard.

"Okay, Blue," he said, mopping up the last of the stew gravy with a thick slice of buttered bread. "We're going to do this your way. Get out the maps and the compass. We'll start from the beginning, mark it all down, and we'll take it all the way to the end."

The end. The last mark. Her eyes lifted to his face, but he'd already jammed his hat back down on his head, and she could see nothing but the line of shadow slanting across his jaw.

"Finish the chocolate. I'll be back in a couple of minutes." Taking the pan and their spoons with him, he scooted over to the tent opening, slipped into his unlaced boots, and disappeared in a gust of wind-driven snow.

Blue stared after him, raising her hand to her cheek and absently brushing away the crystalline flakes he'd allowed inside. He was going to give her the last direction from her father's map, the final clue to her future.

Victory didn't taste sweet at all, she realized amidst more confusion, watching the fire cast his shape against the tent walls. The next day she'd have Lacey's Lode. The next day she'd walk out of his life. There would be no turning back once her deception was complete.

Once you've stolen the treasure out from under him. She gave her head a shake at the blunt thought. She wasn't stealing from him. She was taking what was hers, nothing more, nothing less.

By the time he returned, she'd reconvinced herself of her claim and shut all the mental doors on guilt. She owed him nothing beyond gratitude for her jail release, and a tainted gratitude at best. He'd had his reasons for getting her out—financial reasons.

But those thoughts and convictions proved difficult to hold on to when they were huddled together over the sheaf of maps.

"You're blocking the light. Move back over here," he said, directing her to his side.

Blue ignored him and held her ground, or rather, her edge of sleeping bag. She didn't want to sit next to him, had spent minutes easing herself into a safer position. Walker Evans had an effect on her she was loath to admit even to herself. When he was close, when his arm brushed against hers, or his voice filled her breathing space, she felt overwhelmed on every level. In truth, she was close to hyperventilating in an attempt to remain aloof and calm. She didn't dare get any closer to him.

"Okay, Blue." He let out a long, heavy sigh and sat back on his heels. "What's wrong?"

She gave him a quick once-over, then locked her gaze on the maps spread out between them. *You're too big to get around, especially in this tent; too nice to hate, especially after you've kissed me and warmed my socks; and too good-looking to ignore. In simple terms, you're turning me inside out and backward and I don't know what to do about it.*

"Nothing," she said, fiddling with the compass in what she hoped looked like a competent manner. A large, warm hand under her chin stopped her erratic movements. He tilted her head back, gently forcing her to meet his eyes.

"What is it?" he asked. "The kiss?"

"No—yes . . . I don't know," she stammered, and was immediately embarrassed by the show of weakness. The slow smile curving his mouth did nothing to ease her discomfort.

"Should I kiss you again?" he asked, tracing her lower lip. His eyes darkened and drifted down to follow the lazy path of his thumb. "So you can decide?"

"I'm not even sure I like you," she whispered.

"Yes you are, Blue," he disagreed, his voice softening to an intimate timbre. "I like you too. I like you a lot."

"You don't even know me."

Feeling her tremble beneath his fingers, Walker lowered his hand. "Sometimes I wish I didn't, but the truth is I know you better than you know yourself."

"No."

She sounded so sure, so alone, as if she'd found out long ago she was on her own. He wanted to shake her world a little, make room in there for someone else, make room for himself. "I know you're not a boy, Blue. No matter how big you wear your boots or how short you cut your hair, you're still a woman, a very pretty woman."

She nervously lifted her hand to her nape. "You're a fine one to talk about haircuts. I bet you haven't been to a barber in a year."

"More like three or four," he said, backing off, allowing her to misinterpret the true subject of their conversation. "The man in Walden is a butcher, gave me a cowlick the last time I went to him, and I can't quite bring myself to walk into a beauty parlor. Didn't think I was doing a bad job on my own, though."

"You do that by yourself?" she asked, her head coming up in amazement.

Walker grinned. He wasn't vain, but he knew what he looked like, and he also knew that if he couldn't do a better job than the barber, he would have found the front door of the beauty shop. "A friend taught me how to do it without resorting to using a bowl on my head. It's not too tough once you get the hang of it."

"A lady friend?" Blue asked, the words out before she had time to stop them.

"Yeah, a lady friend. I've had a few. Maybe more than a few."

The disclosure, though spoken without any intent, cast a noticeable pall over her moment of lightness. He watched her lashes lower over her eyes and a deep breath rise in her chest.

"Don't kiss me anymore, Walker, please."

"Sex isn't a dirty word, Blue," he said softly, reaching for her again. "It's a part of life. I can't say I didn't make mistakes when I was young and full of myself. I probably broke a few hearts. Got my own broken more than once. But people grow up; expectations change. Look at me." He brushed her cheek, a light caress asking her to open her eyes. When she did, he stroked his hand across her hair, gently pushing it back. "Just because you haven't found it all, the lifetime commitment, the love that grows instead of fades, doesn't mean you can stop trying. Sometimes we all need to wake up with someone else. Sometimes we all have to settle for caring and warmth instead of love."

"Not me."

Her answer angered him, because he knew it was the truth and he wished for this one night it wasn't. "Why not, Blue? Did your nice boy from Texas turn out to be not so nice after all?"

The instant he spoke, he wished he hadn't. Dammit. She had him going every which way. He could love her tonight, with warmth and tenderness and maybe something more, and never once would he feel that he'd "settled for" anything, but the thought she might was enough to lower his hand from her face. He didn't want to be loved and forgotten by this woman in the way he'd forgotten other women. He would have laughed out loud at himself if he hadn't been so surprised.

"Let's get back to work," he said gruffly, smoothing out the map and giving it his fullest concentration. "Do you have the list?"

Blue reached across her sleeping bag and picked up the piece of notepaper with the directions from the original map written on it. He'd thrown her again, left her with half feelings and thoughts that led her nowhere except into trouble. She wanted him to kiss her. She wanted him to kiss her and never stop. Instead, she'd drawn her line and made him mad.

"We're at forty paces due north," she said.

"Where we were supposed to find 'BRK,' Bear Rock."

"Or something."

"You've got another idea?" He glanced up.

Blue shook her head and wrote "BRK" on her list. One more, she thought, just give me one more.

"Well, as far as I can tell, we haven't taken any wrong turns. The damn thing is supposed to be right here"—he stuck the pencil point on the map—"right where we are. We should be sleeping on it."

Not quite, she thought, silently searching the map from the true starting mark to the point of "BRK." Without her private map, the one she'd worked on every night in her room, the task was difficult, but not impossible. She scanned the peaks and ridges in a five-square-inch area. "What's the last direction?" she asked, her voice deliberately casual.

"Forty paces due north."

"Not the last direction you gave me, the last direction from my father's map," she explained.

"That's it, Blue. Forty paces due north. 'BRK.' Then forty paces due north."

Then she was looking right at it. An unexplainable mixture of anticipation and frustration built inside her as she stared to the left of his pencil. It was right in front of her, in those five square inches of contour lines. She mentally named all the points in the area: Big Horn Gulch; Spring Creek, so named because it only ran in the spring; Wapiti Pass, which was no pass at all; Bays Back Ridge—

Bays Back Ridge. She held her breath for an instant, the name flashing through her mind. There never had been a "BRK." The night he'd crunched her map, he'd admitted to some pieces of wax falling off, and now she knew exactly which pieces he'd destroyed, "BBR" for Bays Back Ridge. The name alone would have meant nothing; Bays Back Ridge was a long stretch of mountaintop covering over a mile of distance, but from the highly detailed approach given by her father, there could be only one particular spot from which to walk the last forty paces.

Closing her eyes, she envisioned the scree slope on the northern side of the ridge, a treacherous slide of rock falling from the westernmost pinnacle, the highest point of the ridge on North Star land. Forty paces on near vertical, shifting slabs of mother earth could put a person anywhere depending on their weight and surefootedness. The hiding place of Lacey's Lode was like a bad joke. A big man with long legs—a man like Walker—could easily end up at the bottom of the hill with forty

paces. With the rock slickened by a covering of
snow, even she would have trouble maintaining
enough balance to count paces instead of the number of feet slid, or—and a tingle of true fear snaked
down her middle at the thought—the number of
feet fallen. She wished they'd brought a rope.

The scree slope of Bays Back Ridge, the map
hidden below the island in Lake Agnes—dammit.
Abel hadn't made his hoard easy to find or even
retrieve once it was found. The location practically proved her long-thought theory that he'd only
put the clues in his will to test her mettle from
the grave. She wondered if he'd known she'd end
up risking her life, first with O'Keefe and now with
the scree slope of the ridge.

Eight

Her face had gone through a myriad of transitions in the minutes since he'd given her the last direction, making Walker wonder what was going on behind her dark eyes, making him uneasy. Now her gaze was transfixed on the map, empty of all but the deepest thoughts. Was she going to confess?

"Blue?" he questioned.

Troubled brown eyes slowly rose to his face, and she spoke quietly. "He didn't make it easy. He made it hard, too hard. I don't think he wanted me to find anything. I don't think he expected me to get this far."

"Of course he did. If he hadn't, we wouldn't be sitting here." Confess? He didn't think so. She sounded ready to give up.

"No, Walker." Her voice shook, and she began rolling up the maps. "He wouldn't have done this to me. He loved me. No matter what . . . no matter what we said to each other sometimes, he loved me."

"I'm sure of it. Look Blue"—he covered her hands with one of his own, lightly, just a touch to let her know he was there—"my dad and I said some pretty harsh things to each other too. Hell, I told you about the night in Gould, the night we really went at each other. That doesn't mean we loved each other less than other sons and fathers, just maybe that we had a harder kind of love, harder to talk about, harder to share, but not less."

She was close to tears, too close, and she had to stop them from coming. "Hard love," she scoffed, pulling away from him and continuing to roll up the map. "I didn't know there was any other kind."

"Your mother?"

"Died."

In the back of his mind Walker had known Sara Dalton had died long ago. As a boy he'd heard the whispers of pity for a little girl, and he remembered his cheeks burning with shame and praying the wags of Walden weren't saying the same things about him and Janelle behind their backs—*practically orphaned, father's a drunk, ranch going into the ground, poor things.* At the time, Mrs. Dalton had only been a name from somewhere up on a ranch in North Park. She hadn't been a flesh and blood woman. She hadn't been the mother of the rare, uniquely feminine creature taking over his life.

But she must have been beautiful, all golden hair and dark eyes, and with the fine mixture of delicacy and strength he found in her daughter's face. Abel had been a fool to go on loving another man's woman.

"Maybe that's what's wrong with us," he said to Blue. "No mother's love to take the rough edges off."

"There's nothing wrong with me," she replied pointedly.

"Sure there is, Blue. You've never given a man a chance. And me? Well, I've given every woman who ever caught my eye only half a chance."

"I don't want to hear about your sex life."

"And I'm not talking about sex. Don't you ever think about getting married and having children of your own?"

"No."

"Liar."

She reacted on pure instinct, her eyes flashing, her hand flying toward his face. He caught her wrist in the split second before she connected, and held her tight.

"Maybe you're right, Blue," he drawled, his eyes flicking to the rolled maps clenched in her other fist. "Maybe we've done enough work for tonight. Tomorrow is going to be another of those long days." He'd given her what she wanted, the last direction. It was up to her what she did with it, and up to him to follow her to the end of the trail.

Blue's breath hurt in her chest. Her wrist hurt under his grip, and she thanked him for both the pain and the anger filling her. He'd hardened her resolve, turned her back into the woman she needed to be—until her lifted her hand to his mouth, touching his lips to her fingers above the frayed ends of her gloves, and turned her back into just a woman.

"You're warm. Good. Get some sleep. I'll be back."

That's what she was afraid of, she realized with

more anger and confusion, more afraid of him than of falling off Bays Back Ridge.

Walker crossed over the campsite and knelt by the fire, slowly pulling on his gloves. They were too much alike. That was the problem. He picked up a stick and poked at the dying embers. He and the lady in the tent had more trouble keeping a conversation civil than any two people he'd ever known. One minute they were talking about love, and in the next—hell, he didn't know what to do with her, except give her time to cool off.

A short whistle from the tent drew his head around, and he watched her dog slip inside. Great, he thought, wet dog. With a muttered curse he jabbed at the fire again, sending a shower of red and gold sparks up into the cloud-filled sky.

Blue rearranged herself in her sleeping bag for the third time, trying and failing to find a comfortable position. Worse, every time she moved, Trapper moved, and she had him right where she wanted him, between her and Walker's sleeping bags.

"Stay," she hissed, pushing him back down. Trapper groaned but settled in beside her. "Good boy."

Tomorrow, Blue. Plan for tomorrow, don't think about tonight. She pushed and shoved her coat into a pillow and nestled her head into its downy comfort. Two deep breaths later her pulse began to slow, and the weariness she'd battled all day finally began to win. *Tomorrow you find your future, your fortune. . . . Walker can . . . who cares what he does? Think of Lacey's Lode, of old sterling falling through your fingers, all yours, of stones brighter than the sky above, of metal worked into beauty and matrix shot through with rich turquoise . . . a treasure hoard hidden in the Sweet Mary by renegades on the run, a treasure found by your father and willed to you. . . .*

Walker watched the last flame flicker and die in the growing darkness of the fire ring. He scooped the accumulated snow off his thigh and squeezed it into a soft, malleable shape. Spring snow, he thought. She could run in the morning —he was going to let her run—but she couldn't hide her tracks, not in the wet stuff Mother Nature had laid on the country.

She'd had plenty of chances to tell the truth, to let him in on the deal, and she'd decided to go it alone. He dropped the snow onto the ground and stood up. She could have it her way, until he caught her with Lacey's Lode in her hands.

He walked back to the tent and let himself inside. The first thing he did was slip out of his boots and slip into his sleeping bag. The second was to look her dog straight in the eyes and say, "Move." He liked dogs as well as the next person, but he didn't fancy sleeping next to a wet one.

When Trapper had found a spot at the bottom of the sleeping bags, Walker rolled onto his side and pulled Blue close. She made a minimum of fuss and actually snuggled up closer, convincing him she was sleeping like a baby. He kept one arm around her middle. He didn't care if she took off in the morning; he just wanted to make damn sure he knew when she left.

Later, much later in the night, he woke to find the tables turned. He was flat on his back, and she had him pinned to the floor. Her head rested in the nook of his shoulder, her soft breaths sighing across his neck. He lay quietly for a long time, holding her and listening to the tent walls quiver in the wind. The silence closer to the ground told him how far up the snow had drifted. The drop in temperature and the shadows rippling across the front of the tent told him the sky had cleared, leaving the full moon free to shine down through the trees.

Ah, Blue, he thought on a deep breath, closing his eyes. *What am I going to do about you?*

Waking to an internal alarm, Blue slowly opened her eyes and took careful stock of her surroundings. The faint light of dawn revealed a large bundle of white fur curled up against the inside curve of her legs. Trapper. She started to reach for him, then found she couldn't move. She turned her head and peeked over the edge of her sleeping bag to where Trapper was supposed to be, and instead saw Walker Evans pressed along the full length of her body from above her head to well past her feet. Mostly she saw his shoulder, but she heard his deep, even breaths filling the quietness, and she felt the warmth of him surrounding her, especially in the strong, muscled arm thrown across her middle. She was trapped.

She pondered the problem for a minute: the logistics, her chances of escaping unnoticed, and the improprieties. They weren't supposed to have gotten this close to each other. Even with two layers of sleeping bag between them, she felt the possessiveness in the angle of his body wrapped half around her. She didn't doubt that he'd corralled her on purpose. Trapper wouldn't have disobeyed a "stay" command unless it had been recanted. Regardless, she had to get out of the tent. Easing one arm up to her neck, she slid the zipper down to her knees.

Walker heard the hushed sound and decided to make things simple for her. With a soft groan he rolled away from her over to the far side of the tent, giving her all the room she needed to run out on him.

Blue held her breath and shot a wary glance at his back. Seconds later she quietly scrambled out of the tent, taking her sleeping bag with her.

The morning was still dark, with only the barest traces of dawn reflecting above the mountains. She didn't waste time starting a fire or fixing breakfast, and probably broke a record stuffing her sleeping bag and tying it onto her backpack. Every step she took would be frozen in the snow pack, an undisguised trail. Her only advantage was time. She had to get in and get out before he caught up with her—*finder's keeper's.*

Silently gesturing to Trapper to follow, she hefted her pack to her back and struck out on the straightest line to Bays Back Ridge, the gray pinnacle of rock backlit by the rising sun in the east.

Walker took his time waking up. He'd accurately predicted her first move of the day, and he didn't doubt his ability to go on staying one step ahead of her even if he was an hour behind her.

But it took him less than an hour to fill his

thermos with hot coffee, down a triple bowl of instant oatmeal, and break camp. And it didn't take any time at all to find her trail.

He kept up a steady, even pace throughout the morning, his strides eating up two of hers with each step. She didn't have a chance, but she didn't seem to be aware of that particular fact. She was melting into the forest almost faster than he could keep up—almost, but not quite.

He followed her tracks to the edge of a meadow and stopped where she'd scuffed the snow. He knelt with one knee on the ground and pushed his hat to the back of his head. His fingers gently lifted the low raspberry branch that had caught his eye. Tufts of white hair clung to the thorns. A canine print was pressed into the snow below the bush. He grunted in satisfaction. The dog was holding up.

His gaze lifted past the raspberry patch to the conifers darkening the ground with morning shadows. Beyond the trees the peaks of the Rawahs cut a jagged line across the sky.

"Where's she taking you, Trapper?" he murmured under his breath, searching the hills, wondering if they'd both be camping out in the snow again tonight. He rose from his kneeling position and brushed the snow off his knee. He could easily catch her before nightfall, but it wouldn't do him much good. She needed to be free. She needed to lead him to Lacey's Lode before he confronted her.

Walker settled his hat lower on his forehead and took up her trail again, not at all sure what he was going to do when he caught her with the goods. Fighting hadn't gotten him anywhere, and he doubted if reason would either. But one thing he did know, he wasn't going to let her get away with it all. In truth, he didn't think he was going to let the lady get away, period.

In mid-afternoon he found himself pacing back and forth through a glade of budding aspens, stopping every couple of steps to check the ground. The melting snow had made a mess of her tracks, but she'd obviously changed her mind about her direction when she'd reached the glen, or maybe she'd made a mistake. Stranger things had been known to happen, but he doubted if they happened to her very often.

More likely, she'd deliberately tracked in and out of the trees to throw him off. Well, she'd have to do better than that to lose him.

Dammit, Blue. He knelt again, found nothing, and moved on. A half an hour later he picked up her trail, his mood sorely deteriorated. Anger lengthened his strides, anger and determination. He'd fooled around with her long enough.

Blue stood at the crest of the ridge, thirty feet below the pinnacle, scanning the downside of the northern slope. The weather had been working against her all day and was having the last laugh. The slight melt of the afternoon had frozen up with the setting sun, turning the scree slope into an ice field. If she'd had it all to do over again, she'd have waited until summer. Who knew how much better things might have gone in July instead of April? Maybe O'Keefe wouldn't have caught up with her, and without O'Keefe there wouldn't have been any tracker named Walker Evans pushing her past sensible limits.

But he was back there, and she was only forty paces away from her fortune. She looked down the mountain again and took a deep breath. She'd have to carry her pack with her, because she doubted if she'd be able to climb back up.

Forty paces into nowhere. There's nothing there. She visually traced a path across the mountain, following a line up to the base of the pinnacle. Then she saw it, a row of crystalline quartz jammed under a flat sheet of shale, the black-and-gray-flecked white chunks almost imperceptible in the snow. They didn't belong on the north side of Bays Back Ridge, and Mother Nature never arranged her playing pieces that neatly.

Excitement, sweet and pure, shot through her, shortening her breath. *Lacey's Lode.* She tightened the hip strap on her pack, pulling it snug.

"Don't follow me, Trapper." She pointed to an easier slope to her right and snapped her fingers. "That way, boy. Go on. Git. I'll meet you at the bottom."

The dog whined, picking up on the agitation in her voice. His paws danced a pattern in the snow, but Blue didn't bother to erase the marks. By the time Walker got to the ridge, she'd be long gone.

Trapper took two steps and stopped, looking back at her.

"Go on. I'll be fine." She urged him forward with a sweep of her hand.

He finally obeyed, almost. He took off, but in the wrong direction, disappearing over the back of the ridge. Blue didn't blame him. He'd chosen the easiest route to the bottom of the hill—the longest, but the easiest. She wasn't worried about him finding his way; shepherds didn't know the meaning of the word lost.

And she didn't want to dwell on the meaning of the word clearheaded, doubting if it applied to her in her current situation. The rocks shifted beneath her feet without any added movement on her part.

Fortifying herself with a long breath, she eased herself off the ridge and onto the scree, keeping her knees bent and her weight angled into the mountain. She slipped once and caught herself. Then she took a second step.

Walker slipped in the gully, caught himself, swore vehemently, and kept going. He'd decided what he was going to do with her, and it started with a good verbal thrashing. Bays Back Ridge; he'd figured it out about an hour ago, and his heart hadn't been quite right since. If the mountain didn't kill her, he just might. She should have trusted him. They could have gone back for ropes and tackled the scree slope with a measure of safety. Instead she'd gone on alone and was probably lying in a pile at the bottom, broken into a hundred pieces by her own damn stubbornness.

The image added force to his next steps. He crawled where he had to and walked when he could, mentally cussing her with every step. Near the top of the cut a sharp bark brought his head up. Trapper came around the side of the mountain alone, and a cold shot of fear went through

Walker. He lost his footing and slid backward a few feet before he caught himself. He grabbed a handful of jagged rock, but didn't feel the edge cut into his fingers or the warm blood run into his palm.

Scrambling faster than made good sense, he double-timed his way up to the top of the ridge. And the closer he came, the more his fear increased.

Blue wedged herself under the slab of shale, swearing at the cold, the unsteady earth beneath her, and the dying sun above. One by one, she dug the chunks of quartz away from their resting places and sent them rolling and bouncing down the slope. The vast silence of the dusk swallowed up the retreating sounds of rock hitting rock. Her hand brushed against something soft, something that didn't belong in the harsh landscape of snow, earth, and stone.

She stopped all movement for a second, believing but not believing she'd finally found the stuff of her dreams. Then she slowly ran her fingers over what she couldn't see: folds of canvas, two leather straps, the cold metal of a buckle. Her chin dropped to her chest, lowered by a rising tide of emotion, a mix of elation and sadness. She'd found Lacey's Lode; she'd come to the end. She tugged the heavy bundle into the open air and clasped it close to her chest for a long, quiet moment.

The twilight shadows slipped up her body and washed over the rocks, reminding her of her need for haste. Time enough for looking later, she told herself, but years of anticipation overruled the logic of her thoughts.

With fingers numb from the cold she unbuckled the straps, promising herself she'd only look once, quickly, then be on her way. If she waited now, she'd have to wait longer, until—she didn't know when. She didn't know if she'd make camp tonight or try for Walden. She couldn't think beyond the bundle in her lap. She tried not to think at all about the man behind her. She unwound the straps, visually measuring the encroaching darkness and praying it would hold off long enough to give her one look at her hard-won treasure.

Parts of the canvas tore as she unfolded the cloth, falling away, rotten and worn. Each of the pieces was individually protected in soft, thin leather, and she would have unwrapped one of them first if something else hadn't caught her eye—a sheet of paper tucked amid the separate packages.

Curiosity tinged with a different, special kind of excitement guided her hand in pulling it free. Her fingers shook, making the paper tremble . . . *a message from her father.* He'd left her a message. He'd believed in her, had believed she'd find Lacey's Lode. She forced herself to calm down, to keep the paper still long enough to read the words scrawled across the lined sheet.

But it didn't take many of the words, four or five at the most, before she realized all of her other mistakes were nothing compared to the one she'd made by believing in her father. Abel had never wanted her to find his damn treasure. He'd never wanted her at all. The letter was to Lacey, to Lacey and the son she'd had by another man, the son who should have been his.

An icy, mind-paralyzing calmness seeped into her consciousness, and with the greatest of care she rewrapped the bundle, her anger showing only in the extra force she used to tighten the straps. She debated whether or not to shove the damn thing back under the rock and let him find it on his own, then decided against such a churlish reaction. She'd lost; he'd won, fair and square.

Cradling the package in her lap, she leaned back against the rock and watched the night steal the last light from the sky, and she waited for Walker Evans to come and claim what was his.

Nine

"Blue!"

She heard him call her name from up above on the ridge, but didn't move to respond in any way.

"Blue! Are you hurt?" he hollered again.

Yes, she was hurt, deep down inside. Damn all men. She'd been right never to trust a one of them. She clutched the canvas bag closer to keep herself from throwing it down the mountain—or worse, ripping it open again and rereading the letter. *The son who should have been his, Walker Evans.*

Stifling a groan of pure frustration and anger, she held the package even closer. Her whole life had been a lie. She'd lost and had nowhere to go from there. Everything she'd worked for belonged to him, to the one man who had caught her.

A small avalanche tumbled down the mountain, skittering by her to the right, preceding his approach. "Dammit it, Dalton! Talk to me!"

"When hell freezes over," she hissed, squeezing

her eyes closed. Of all of them, he'd proven to be the worst, playing her along, being nice to her, with those damn kisses of his. He hadn't fooled her, but she'd come close to fooling herself.

Suddenly she didn't want to face him, not when she was hurting, not when she'd lost. She started to rise, but he caught her from behind, whirling her around and causing them both to slide another ten feet down the ridge.

Walker pulled her close, stopping them both more with the force of his will and anger than his balance. Standing below her, he gripped her arms and shook her, shouting in her face. "What in the hell kind of damn fool—you could have—what is it with you? A death wish?"

"You're hurting me," she said through gritted teeth. He had no more claim on her time, and she had no more time for midnight dreams, naive wishes, and memories she couldn't forget. He didn't belong to her. Nothing belonged to her.

"I ought to—I ought to—" He gave up in frustration and shook her again, once, hard, forcing her to look at him. "You've gone too far this time, Blue. Too damn far. You can shoot at me all you want, threaten me with that damn big knife you carry, but if you ever pull a stunt like this again, I'll chain you to the cabin wall. *I swear I will.*"

His ultimatum snapped her control. She glared back at him through the deepening twilight. "You're not my keeper! Nobody tells me—" She struggled to pull her arm free and sent them into another pell-mell slide.

He didn't release her as they both scrambled to gain a foothold and went farther down the mountain. Boots slipped on the icy rocks, hands reached for something to hold on to besides each other, but he didn't let her go. The package she'd been holding made it to the bottom before they did, but neither of them noticed.

"I'm telling you! And I'm only telling you once!"

"You're telling me nothing!" Blue landed on her bottom, her fall cushioned by her sleeping bag and his leg. She fought to gain her release.

Walker was having none of it. He got to his feet and pulled her up right along with him. He brushed the snow off her, none too gently, all the while maintaining his grip on her arm. "We're going home. If you've still got enough energy to fight when we get there, maybe you are a better man than me. Until then, I want you to head your nose down the trail. We're not too far from the North Star . . . but I guess you knew that all along." *Damn you,* he added silently to himself. *Damn you for lying to me, for taking the ridge alone, for not trusting me. And damn you most of all for putting your life in danger when I was right there to help you.* "Don't forget your junk." He picked up the canvas bundle and shoved it in her arms, his actions and his words heavily laden with the fury he was trying to control.

Too furious herself to speak, Blue stalked off through the trees, instinctively heading in the right direction. Trapper caught up with them within the first hundred yards, the only one of them too smart to take the ridge.

Their angry silence became a palpable presence in the dark, quiet forest. Steps were taken on long strides, heads were held high, branches were broken underfoot with total disregard for marking or finding a trail. She had nothing left to hide but the ownership of the package she held in her arms, and she had no intention of doing that. She stopped and turned suddenly and shoved it into his midsection with a thud. *"Carry your own junk."*

Walker barely kept the bundle from falling to the ground, but he didn't question her statement. He was too busy trying not to yell at her all the way down the mountain. The woman was going to be the death of him, but he still didn't want to let her go. He should be running in the opposite direction as fast as his feet could carry him. Instead he was following her through the night and wishing he had enough courage to ask her to give him her backpack to carry. He could just imagine what kind of response he'd get, and he wasn't up for any more of her stubbornness or her colorful language.

At the truck she flung open the door and slammed it shut. Walker got behind the wheel. Blue no sooner had gotten her door closed than she opened it again.

"Stay put," Walker ordered, getting out of the truck. "I'll help him."

Blue closed her door again and waited while Walker lifted her dog into the bed of the truck. She would have helped Trapper with a boost; Walker just picked him up and set him down inside.

He got back in the cab and slammed his door, too, letting her know she was far from being off the hook. Nothing about the ride home appeased either of them, not the cold, the constant bouncing and jostling, or the bundle of "junk" nestled between them on the seat.

He brought the truck to one last bone-jarring halt in front of the cabin and got out without a word. Fine, Blue thought, her mouth grim. She had no intention of fighting with him, or even speaking with him. She was getting the rest of her stuff and getting out.

Once inside the cabin she wasted no time hauling all of her things to the front door, and he let her, without a word of disagreement. When she had it all piled up, she walked into the kitchen, studiously ignoring the canvas bag he'd thrown on the dining table. Curiosity had no place in her life. She wanted, needed, a clean break. To give in to the lure of Lacey's Lode once more would be a final act of foolishness she was determined not to commit. The lure of Walker Evans didn't even bear thinking about.

"I'd like to borrow your car . . . please." The request came hard, the politeness harder still. "I'll leave it in Walden."

"Be my guest," he replied curtly, handing her the key behind his back without even a glance.

She had one more thing to clear up, just so there wouldn't be any misunderstanding. "There's a letter in the package. Lacey's Lode belongs to you. It always belonged to you. I won't be back, and I won't try to get any of it for myself." The noble words stuck in her craw, but she'd be damned if she let him see her for the chump she'd been played for by her father. If nothing else, she'd walk out of there with her pride.

"Fine." He didn't give a damn about any letters, and at his point he didn't care who Lacey's Lode belonged to.

"Fine." She stomped out of the kitchen and out of the cabin with the key in her hand.

Ten minutes later she stomped back in. The sound of the shower drew her unerringly to the bathroom. She pounded on the door. "Walker! Your car won't start!"

"What?"

She cracked the door open and was met by a wall of steam. "I said your car doesn't work!"

"I know." His voice was muffled by the running water and the shower curtain, but Blue heard him.

"What do you mean, you know?"

"It never starts in weather below forty degrees. *Never,*" he added for emphasis.

"Then why—"

"You're a smart lady. You figure it out." He cut her off, and she heard the water stop and the shower curtain being pulled back. She quickly ducked out and slammed that door too.

In the living room she was immediately confronted with the canvas bag lying on the table. He hadn't touched it. The cloth was wet where the snow had melted in little pools, undisturbed by a human hand. The leather straps were still cinched tight.

Trusting fool . . . It would be so easy to take it away from him, to grab the bag and run. She swore softly. Maybe he did know her better than she knew herself. A part of her desperately wanted to take what should have been hers, but underneath the desperation lay her pride. She didn't want Walker Evans to think her a thief, and she didn't want him coming after her.

No, she thought on a heavy sigh, lowering her chin to her chest and briefly closing her eyes. She didn't want him coming after her again. Twice was enough. He'd won, and she was right back where she'd started from, broke and alone. In truth, more alone than she'd been before—before he'd kissed her, before he'd shared his home with her.

Get out, Blue. Get out before you miss what you have no right to want. The search was over, and all she'd found was more of what she needed and less of what she could have. Walker Evans, with his passionate kisses and strong arms, wasn't for her. His life revolved around the mountains and the seasons, her mountains, the seasons she felt changing with every sunrise, but he wasn't for her.

She slumped against the back of the couch, splaying her legs and letting her hands fall to her lap. The muscles in her thighs began to tremble, and she planted her boots more firmly on the floor, trying to stop the outward sign of physical weakness. He'd pushed her too hard, too damn hard. Her gaze slid to the hallway. *Go, Blue. Go. There's nothing here for you.*

But she didn't leave. She waited, and she watched the hall, and she fought her silent battle of loss and need, of impossible want and painful denial. Love didn't enter into her equation. Her experience with the emotion had been too limited for her even to begin to work with it. Love was a labyrinth, and no one had ever given her a good, reliable map.

A moment later he emerged from the bathroom, still buttoning his jeans, a towel draped around his neck. She pushed off the couch and retreated farther into the living room, turning her back on him. One look had been enough.

"May I borrow your truck . . . please." Politeness didn't come any easier with practice, especially with him half naked behind her. She'd caught a glimpse of his tight abdomen and the golden shade of his skin, and all the hard muscle beneath both, and her mouth had gone a bit dry, making it hard to sound as angry as she was trying to feel.

"No." He strode by her, barefoot, seemingly oblivious to the effect he was having on her. His jeans weren't tight, not nearly tight enough. She was afraid any second they might slip off his hips. The slight gap between the cloth and his body drew her attention with each step he took. And when he returned from the kitchen with a cup of coffee, she found her gaze riveted to a hand's span of distance above his jeans, the distance between where a silky arrow of sable hair started at his navel to where it disappeared beneath the soft gray-blue denim. A heat she didn't feel on the outside built inside, flushing her cheeks.

"I . . . I can't walk out of here tonight, Walker. I'm too tired."

He knew that. He could tell just by looking at her, and it made him mad all over again. "Then I guess you're going to have to wait until I'm ready to take you."

"When will that be?" Dark eyes lifted from his stomach to his eyes. He felt the slow rise of her gaze like a touch. He felt the effort it cost her. He knew what she was thinking; it was written in the soft parting of her mouth, in the weakness she was fighting, and that, too, made him mad.

"Maybe tomorrow morning. Probably not."

"Why?" she asked, confusion evident in the slight

tilt of her head, a confusion he wasn't buying anymore.

"You know why, Blue. Go take your shower, get warm, get into dry clothes, then I'll take care of your face."

"What's wrong with my face?" She lifted a hand to her cheek and winced at the tender bruise she found.

There were a lot of things wrong with her face, mostly that looking at it broke his heart. A face like hers should have been framed by something soft and pretty instead of layers of worn-out flannel, a ragged old cowboy hat, and a faded bandana. He, who had always known what his looks were and what they could get him, and found it not much of lasting importance, had fallen in love with a woman who didn't know she was beautiful.

"I left plenty of hot water," he said gruffly, and turned back into the kitchen.

Blue pulled her hat off her head and dragged a hand through her hair. There was no winning anymore, not in her life. She was cold from the inside out and the outside in. Her body was bruised and battered, stretched to its limit, and she'd left the last of her spirit halfway down Bays Back Ridge. She needed more than a shower to put things right, but it was probably the only thing she was going to get. Sighing, she dropped the hat on the end table and turned wearily toward the bathroom.

When she was clean, warm, and dry, everything he'd told her to be, she flicked off the bathroom light and prepared herself to face him. She knew what she had to do and hoped she had enough guts and civility left in her to do it without making a bigger mess of everything.

He was seated at the kitchen table, sprawled back in a chair with one leg up on the table. The riches of Lacey's Lode were spread out in front of him, a tarnished mélange of sterling silver and fine turquoise. Firelight reflected the dull shine of a squash-blossom necklace tangled in his fingers, the delicate workmanship contrasting with the weathered roughness of his hands. She followed the piece as he lowered it to the table, then, un-bidden, her gaze drifted to the arch of his bare foot. Her eyes traced the curve up his leg and thigh to the forest-green shadows of his shirt and the bronze highlights in his hair. The play of light in the darkened corner of the room made him appear half real and bigger than life. The tight expression on his face added to the intimidating illusion. One piercing glance from his narrowed eyes told her it was no illusion. The man was madder than hell and barely controlling the emotion.

Expediency and escape, she decided, were her best moves. "I want to apologize."

"Then do it."

The harshness of the command took her by surprise, but she struggled forward with the words she'd memorized under the shower spray. "I shouldn't have lied to you. I know I wasted a lot of your time, and I'm sorry, but in my position you would have done the same thing."

"I was in your position, and that's not good enough."

To hell with civility, she thought, feeling the hackles rise on the back of her neck. "I'm trying to apologize, and you won it all. That's going to have to be good enough," she spoke each word succinctly, her hands clenched at her sides.

"You're not even close." He swung his leg to the floor and slowly rose, his hands gripping the edge of the table.

"I don't know what in the hell else you expect of me, and I really don't give a damn."

"Expect?" His voice lowered to a dangerous level. "I'll tell you what I expected."

"Sorry. I'm fresh out of time. I've decided I do have the strength to leave tonight, with or without your help."

"You're not running out on me again, Blue." He came around the table, and she backed off a step.

"The hell I'm not." She wasn't afraid of him, but neither was she a fool.

"I'm tired of fighting with you, and I'm through with giving you enough rope to hang yourself." He came closer with each statement, stalking her slowly across the room. "Your face is scratched and bruised. You look like a strong wind would blow you away, and if you think you can throw a few trinkets at me and walk out of my life, you better think again."

"Trinkets?" She felt the couch on the backs of her legs and stopped, forcing her head up to meet his gaze.

He didn't stop coming until he'd passed all the boundaries of personal space and common courtesy, until his thighs brushed against hers, until he towered over her and held her chin in the palm of his hand. Golden flames reflected in his eyes, burning away the last of her courage. Her pulse began to race and her muscles to quiver.

"I *expected* you to be rough around the edges, and you are," he said, growling. "I *expected* you to be trouble, and you're more than I bargained for. I *expected* you to tell the truth, and you didn't. And somehow, Blue"—he rubbed his thumb over her bottom lip, slowly, ever so slowly, and his voice lowered to a desperately soft drawl—"somehow, through all of it, despite most of it . . . somehow, I *expected* this. . . ." His voice trailed off as he lowered his mouth to hers and pressed her back against the couch, flanking her with his long, hard legs.

The blatantly sexual action stole her breath and made her knees weaken. The tender invasion of his tongue into her mouth sent a wave of heat pouring down her body to settle between her thighs. She sunk against him, wrapping her fingers around the waistband of his jeans to keep from falling.

Walker wasn't going to let her fall. He held her with his hand at her nape. He held her with his arm around her back, reveling in the enchantment of her sweet mouth and the even sweeter pressure of her small, strong body against his. Beneath the rough edges, past all the trouble, lay the woman he'd dreamed her to be, warm and passionate, uniquely formed to give him pleasure.

He moved his mouth over hers and felt her rise against him, molding her soft curves to his hard angles. He lifted her higher into his arms, one hand sliding down her leg and wrapping it around his waist. Behind his back he tugged her boot off and let it fall to the floor, and he pressed harder into her.

"Ah, Blue," he said with a groan, laying a path of kisses up the contour of her cheek to her hairline. He buried his face in the thick flaxen strands, shifting her weight against him and working off her other boot. "Say yes."

The raw need in his voice shot through her with heart-stopping intensity. She heard her boot fall, and she felt the hot warmth of his breath on her neck, sensitizing her skin and making her yearn for more. His hand on the buttons of her shirt, and the remnants of her pride, compelled her to speak before she forgot who he was, the son her father never had.

"Walker . . . no."

"Yes, Blue." He lifted his head and bracketed her face in his large hands. The callused pads of his thumbs traced the tender skin below her eyes; his palms cupped her cheeks. "You're staying tonight, staying with me. No posse is going to ride up and take you away. Your dog isn't going to rescue you. There's only me, and I'm not letting you go."

She listened to his proclamation, breathless, feeling his hand slide down her throat and pause just above the opening of her shirt. The heat of his touch spread across her chest, and farther when he pushed the first button through its hole. "Please don't."

"Please don't what, Blue? Please don't want you? Impossible." The second button slipped open. "Please don't make you want me? That's almost too easy, isn't it?" He freed the third button, then the fourth. "Or are you trying to say please don't leave me, Walker? Don't steal my dreams and push me back out into the world alone? Well, I'm sorry, Blue, but I am going to steal your dreams. I'm going to steal your kisses, and if I get lucky tonight, real lucky, I'm going to steal your heart the same way you've stolen mine."

"I haven't stolen anything," she whispered, thoroughly aware of what he was doing with her clothes and unable or unwilling to stop him. The distinction seemed beyond her, the decision even more so. He was moving too fast for her to keep up with logic, and her instincts hadn't recovered from his kiss.

"Yes you have. You've stolen my time, but every hour with you is twice as good as the hours without you. You've stolen my privacy and the loneliness of my days"—he freed the final button, his hands lingering where the cloth gaped before disappearing inside her jeans—"and my nights, Blue, what you've stolen from my nights is unforgivable. You've filled them with crazy thoughts and a deep-down ache only you can heal. Fight yourself if you have to, but I know you can't fight me." He tugged her shirt out of her pants and slowly spread it open, his hands brushing across her breasts. As he held her gaze his eyes half-closed in longing and his jaw slackened with a shallow breath. His unconcealed desire filled her with the same deep-down ache he'd confessed. It welled up inside her, dragging panic in its wake.

"I don't want to feel like this . . . to want you," she said, desperate to explain. "I don't want to give myself away."

"Then let me give myself to you," he urged softly. "You can take, Blue. I'll give you everything. Nothing I've got is doing me any good if I keep it to myself." Still holding her gaze, he slid his palms up to cup her breasts, the roughness of his hands moving over the satin of her skin. Then he lowered his eyes and released his breath on a ragged sigh. "Lord, you're pretty, Blue."

When he whispered his soft words, Blue knew

why she had waited. Through all their days together, and all their nights close but apart, she'd dreamed of him saying those words again. No trace of a lie echoed in his deep voice, no hidden reservations obscured the reverence in his eyes. The gift alone weakened her need to fight what she felt when he caressed her. She'd tried so hard all her life not to need anyone, to protect herself from the pain of loving. She'd carved out a narrow space to hold herself and her goal, but Walker Evans had been slowly, surely, chipping her walls away. She wanted to hate him for making her feel her loneliness.

But he touched her, and when he touched her, she had no room for the hate, only the want of more of him. His lips teased her doubts away, gnawing a tantalizing trail back to her mouth, where he captured her for his own. She didn't want to be alone any longer, for reasons she didn't understand. Walker had become the man she needed.

"Hold me, Blue. Make me believe you want me," he commanded huskily, reaching down and releasing the snaps on his shirt one by one.

The heated silkiness of his skin and the hard muscles bunching in his chest teased the peaks of her breasts, and when he tossed his shirt aside and pulled her close, crushing her against him, the teasing turned to wanton need.

She tunneled her fingers through the length of his hair, pulling him back to her open mouth for her kiss. She took what she wanted, the special taste of him, musky-sweet and all male. She gave in to his strength, the graceful power of muscle tightening his arms, gliding in rhythms designed to steal her breath and fill her with wonder.

Walker groaned, feeling her response wash through him like a promise of the loving to come. She said yes with every sweet stroke of her tongue, with every move of her body against him. He gathered her close and, letting her ride his hips, started the long walk from the relative safety of the living room to the bedroom, where there would be no second chances, not this time.

Blue wrapped her legs tighter around his waist and sunk into the magic of his mouth. He bit her lower lip, softly, gently, then laved the tender flesh with his tongue, tasting himself on her. She ran her hands through his hair, pushing it away from the face that had stolen the peace from her nights. If nothing else, she'd leave knowing whether or not her dreams had lied to her about him, and for that she was willing to pay the price he demanded.

Ten

Walker sat down on the bed and, still kissing her, reached over and turned on the lamp, filling the room with pale light. His hands came back to her neck, his thumbs pressing on the underside of her jaw and angling her mouth across his for the deeper thrusts of his tongue. She pressed her body against him, melting into his arms with a woman's warmth.

He slid his hands across her shoulders and down her arms, taking her shirt with them, enchanted by the suppleness of lean muscle and silky skin he revealed. She belonged to him like the mountains and the sky, and he would have all of her.

The soft gasps escaping her lips echoed all the way down his body and tightened the ache building in his loins. He needed more of her, and he took it, rolling her onto her back and tracing a long, wet path to her breasts. He didn't hesitate; he didn't tease. His mouth closed around one rose-tinted peak, applying a gentle suction. His teeth grazed her, his tongue explored, and beneath him he felt her surrender to the same sweet pleasure intoxicating him.

Blue spread her hands wide and let them drift across his shoulders. His slow, languorous nuzzling of her breasts made her body tremble. He left no place on her skin untouched, and he left a fire behind with every intimate kiss, a fire the moistness of his mouth did nothing to assuage. The power of his arms lifted her higher, dragging her across his body as he pulled her on top of him and reclaimed her lips. Lower, she felt him rubbing up against her in a rhythm to match the sweeping strokes of his tongue. The undulating pattern of his hips increased as he opened his legs and let her slip between his thighs. His hands cupped her derriere, holding her against him, moving her until she picked up the irresistible rhythm.

Suddenly she understood the meaning of the word erotic. It was a total assault on the senses. He wore her inhibitions away, taking her with him into a fantasy realm of sensation where the treasures of life were the warming heat of skin touching skin and the soft explosions he relayed to her body with each added degree of pressure.

She became lost in the rocking motion, sliding against him and on top of him, and always wanting more. Of its own accord her hand moved down his hard, muscled chest. She'd never known the sensitivity of her fingertips until they discovered the satin texture of his skin and the ridges of his ribs, until they delved lower and trailed across his stomach. She lingered, letting her palm absorb the rise and fall of the taut plane, letting the heat of him seep into her pores. And as she touched him, as she traced the miracle of corded muscle and soft skin, of heavy heartbeats and pulsing life that was Walker Evans, she knew she'd found something more valuable than the riches of Lacey's Lode in Lacey's son.

"Keep going," he murmured against her lips, bringing her out of her thoughts and back to reality.

She hadn't realized they'd stopped kissing, but their mouths barely met between soft inhalations of air. He'd gone very still beneath her, his body tense in anticipation of her boldness. When she didn't respond to his huskily voiced command, he took her hand in his.

"Making love with me isn't a mistake, Blue, even if I'm not a nice boy from Texas," he whispered, kissing her once more, tasting her lips with a gentle stroke. "Hell, I was never even a nice boy from Colorado. . . ." His voice trailed off as he teased a wet kiss into her palm, slowly unraveling her senses and sending a frisson of heat up her arm. His gaze held hers with a golden fire, somber and intense. When her skin was damp and warm, and her chest hurt from the breath she couldn't take, he slid her hand under his waistband and began unbuttoning his jeans.

"Walker!" she gasped his name.

"Shh, Blue. Just touch me." He moved beneath her, whispering soft words of love along with her name.

She couldn't comply with his intimate request, though she longed for it as much as he, but no such problem stayed him. Blue felt his hands move to her pants. She heard the snap break and the zipper give way. His rough hands slid under the denim, and then under cotton, cupping her with palms. He pulled her down; they touched, and liquid heat poured through her. His low groan mingled with hers as he captured her mouth once more and slowly started the rhythm anew. The wildness and power of him inflamed her senses, sent her reeling. He rolled her beneath him and pressed her deeply into the bed, taking the control she no longer needed.

Her subtle concession required no forethought; the thoughts came tumbling after—thoughts of trust, and Walker, giving and receiving in turn. They drifted and melded with the purely physical excitement he created. They twined with her emotions into a single strand of love.

Love. The truth echoed deep in her heart with a painful longing unlike any she'd ever felt. Her eyes came open on a sharp breath, and she started to pull away, but he caught her and held her fast.

"What's wrong?" he asked, trying and failing to conceal his frustration. His body hurt with needing to be inside her. He couldn't lose her. If he didn't hold her to him now, he'd never be able to hold her. She'd be gone, and this time he'd have to let her go.

Everything was wrong. She felt betrayed by her own sense of values. She'd told him once she wouldn't settle for sex without love, and he'd made her want him, want him so badly, she ached and her love had no more places to hide. He'd stripped away her defenses, left her vulnerable to truths she didn't want to accept.

"Blue, tell me," he insisted, the roughness of his voice softened by the gentleness of his touch.

"I . . . I might be a virgin," she stammered, not lying but neither telling him her real fear.

"Might?"

She nodded, sending a fall of short blond hair down the side of her face, and Walker sighed heavily. He'd done some pretty wild things with women in his life that would leave the question up for grabs, technically, but he didn't want to give the Texas boy that much credit for imagination. He really didn't.

"Did he hurt you?"

"No," she murmured, casting her eyes down, but what she saw only increased her agitation. Walker was beautiful. "He . . . he didn't force me or anything. There was an awful lot of fumbling around, and I never did quite figure it all out."

"Obviously." A wry grin lifted a corner of his mouth as he brushed her cheek with his hand. "I'm not forcing you either, Blue."

"I know."

"But I want you very badly." A patent understatement if he'd ever spoken one. He wanted her crying out his name. He wanted her bound to him with a thousand living ropes of desire and need and love, of tenderness and care, of shared days and nights of comfort beyond passion.

"I know," she whispered so softly, the words were more breath than sound.

He loved her, too, but caution told him to keep the fact to himself. He didn't want to scare her off, and if the truth be known, he hardly believed it himself. But he felt love when he looked at her. The dark wings of her eyebrows framed eyes he wanted to find himself in come morning. The slight body resting beneath his promised to hold more of the earthly delights to be found between a man and a woman than he'd ever found before—

because she was Blue Dalton, the only woman who'd ever captured him with a single kiss. By the time he'd kissed her again, his heart had been long gone down the trail of no return.

"I'm going to be very careful with you," he said, his lips seeking and finding the pulse point in her neck, his hips grinding softly against her, rekindling the flames. "Very . . . very . . . very careful." His voice picked up the cadence of his body, and Blue found herself sinking once more into the desirous magic of his touch. Reason and fear fled before the onslaught of his skilled seduction.

Their jeans became an intolerable barrier for Walker. He couldn't get enough of her, get close enough. He slowed the kiss and the pumping of his body, knowing he was too close to the end to make it good for her. She did things to him, crazy things, with her hesitations and her sweet capitulations. Moment by moment, with every caress of her hands on his body, he felt her come closer to the boundary between shy curiosity and the sheer driving force he'd already given in to. He'd never had trouble waiting for a woman before, but even half clothed she made him restless, made him long for the completion he'd find only when he filled her.

He teased her and played with her, his hands straying ever lower between her thighs. Need pushed him even further, until she met him with an involuntary arch of her hips. A soft moan died unfinished as he took her one step higher, showing her the beginning of the special delight awaiting her. Then, as if she finally understood what he wanted, what he needed from her, she slid her small hand between their bodies. Suddenly he was the one being teased. He took it as long as he could, letting her discover him until he pulsed in her hand with an urgency he could no longer deny.

"Help me, Blue," he whispered, pushing them both to a sitting position and pulling her to the edge of the bed. He got up and shucked off his pants, then pulled her to her feet. "Kiss me."

She did, but barely caught his lips with her own before he slipped away, running his mouth in a wet trail down her body as he dropped to his knees. The gentle, gnawing path excited every inch of her; the touch she'd never imagined had her sinking back onto the bed, her body molten with throbbing pleasure.

"Remember that," he growled huskily, tugging her pants off her feet. Then he started back up, teasing the skin behind her knees and sliding his tongue up her inner thigh.

She was mindless with need, burning up with the anticipation he'd so quickly taught her. She didn't have long to anticipate, to want. He found her again and again, and he felt her melt beneath his mouth. The trembling sweetness of her pushed him to the limits of his control. But he held himself back one minute more, and another, luxuriating in the taste of her and in his own pleasure, until he felt tension tighten her body and in the next second give completely away.

Groaning in satisfaction, he worked his way back up to her mouth, wrapping his arm around her and carrying her to the top of the bed.

Blue held on to him tightly, so tightly. She needed to know he was real. She needed his touch, his kiss, to keep her world right. She hadn't known such feelings existed in herself.

But when she felt him pushing against her, slipping inside of her, she jerked her mouth away. "Don't, Walker, please . . . I can't take anymore." Her body was still pulsing too strongly in the aftermath of his first wild assault.

"Yes you can," he hissed between his teeth, trying to be gentle, and sliding ever deeper. "You can take me. . . . *Take me, Blue.*"

And she did, until she could take no more of his hardness, no more of his length. Walker moaned and thrust deeply, capturing her gasp of pain in his mouth. In the back of his mind he realized what he'd done, but there'd been no stopping the fever-pitch tide of his need. There was no stopping it now. He couldn't pull away, but he could try, really try to ease the invasion.

"Don't move," he whispered, his voice raw. He held her head in his hands, kissing her brow, her cheeks, the side of her nose. "You won't hurt again, I promise, Blue. I promise."

He could have said he was sorry, but he wasn't. He could have said they hadn't known for sure, but it wouldn't have made any difference if they had. The pain was a woman's to bear when she made love the first time. There was nothing he could or would have done differently. He'd wanted all of her; he'd taken all of her. He'd never intended less, but he did intend oh so much more.

Slowly, when he felt her relax in his arms, he began to withdraw, but not completely. The instant flash of wariness in her eyes brought a smile to his face. The challenge of loving her almost equaled the pleasure—almost, but not quite. Her skin was dewy with perspiration, glowing with the exertion of her release. Her eyes were dark, like midnight, bathing him with the desire he felt building in her again.

"You are beautiful, Annabelle Blue"—his smile faded as she moved with him, ever so slightly, reigniting the fire—"and so perfect . . . so tight." He leaned down and whispered a few soft words in her ear, and Blue felt an all-consuming blush race up her body. "Do you understand?" he asked, sliding into her again.

The muscles in his arms flexed on either side of her, banding her with tensile, golden steel. Yes, she understood. He'd already shown her the place he wanted her to reach again—this time with him deep inside her.

She watched the tawny length of his hair fall over his shoulders as he moved above her. She watched his eyes darken and grow heavy lidded with the increasing force of his need, and somewhere between the beauty of him and the wonder of him, she felt passion catch her again.

He filled her, taking her higher with each thrust until she gasped and moaned. He was right; she *was* tight, tight with an inescapable need, strung out to the ends of the earth. Her eyes drifted closed as she tried to find release from the pleasure he gave.

"No, no," he whispered savagely, running his hands through her hair and tilting her head back. "Look at me, Blue. Look at me. I love you. *I love* . . ." His last word disappeared in a mighty groan, but she didn't need to hear those words again. He'd seared them on her heart. Her body pulsed with the fierce pledge, with him deep inside her where he belonged. Her eyes closed, but she still saw him, all golden fire and fulfilled promise.

Walker collapsed on top of her, shuddering, sated. His world had changed irrevocably. Many women had loved him well. No woman had ever loved him like Blue Dalton, she of the wild heart and untamed soul.

His mouth roamed up the side of her face, tenderly, gently. He rolled them onto their sides and held her, kissed her until she calmed in his arms.

"Are you okay?" he asked, brushing the damp hair back off her face.

"Yes," she murmured.

He paused to kiss her cheek and gather her close. "And are you mine, Blue?"

"Yes, Walker." *Tonight I am yours. For the rest of my life I'll remember this night and be yours.*

Walker awoke before dawn, nudged to consciousness by a sense of unease. She was still with him. He felt her slender arm draped across his chest, the warmth of her legs tangled with his. He'd won . . . and he'd lost. She'd surrendered her body, but he'd be a fool to think he'd gotten her everlasting trust and undying devotion. He knew what wasn't said was usually more important than what was, and she had said damn little after the most incredible sexual experience of his life. Worse, he knew what he'd wanted her to say: all those softly murmured declarations from the lips of other women he'd taken if not exactly for granted, not exactly too seriously either. Ego strokes.

She'd stroked him all right—and his body grew heavy even with the memory—but his ego wasn't even in the running. He'd wanted to capture her and instead ended up sinking deeper into the trap she hadn't set. He needed to think.

He rose and settled the blankets back around her body, deliberately not touching her more than necessary. In the living room he stopped and stoked up the fire to take the chill out of the air. He'd slipped into his jeans and now found his shirt where he'd tossed it on the floor.

The cabin was quiet, peaceful in the darkness of predawn. He moved toward the kitchen with the ease of instinct, finding his way by the beginning glimmers of firelight. Outside, the land lay soundless, covered with muted, rolling shades of palest gray and midnight-blue. Snow rounded off the edges of the meadows where they met tree line and blended the peaks into the horizon, smudging the delineation between earth and sky.

He stood over the sink, running water into the coffee pot, and then he waited through the whole brewing process, drop by quiet drop, watching the night.

Blue roused to a gentle kiss and found herself being gathered into his strong arms, quilt and all.

"Walker?" she murmured, not quite coming awake.

"Shh, Blue." He kissed her again, lifting her and holding her against his chest. "I want to watch the sunrise with you, but you can sleep."

Crazy man, she thought, yawning and snuggling her head into the crook of his neck. Crazy, wonderful man.

Walker carried her into the living room and settled them both into the big leather chair in front of the fireplace. In minutes she'd fallen back asleep. He didn't care. He still didn't know what to say. He'd just needed her close, needed to know she was still with him.

When next she awoke, it was to considerably more stimulation. He tasted of coffee, and she slid her arms around his neck as his hand caressed her most vulnerable places beneath the blanket. Neither said a word when he lowered her to the floor and slipped out of his pants and into her. Her body welcomed him, all of him, with each filling stroke. The loving was sweet, gentle, without the tumult of the previous night. He nuzzled her neck, his hair falling across her cheek and throat in silky waves to match the quickening of his pace and her heart. She met him with soft moans and a total relinquishing of self.

This time she was his; Walker felt the truth in the sheer simplicity of her response. He led; she followed. He took; she gave, until she took what he wanted most to give her, the rush of her release. His own climax came easily, so easily within her.

After a long moment he brushed his mouth across her cheek. "Good morning."

"Good morning," she whispered, and he felt the curve of her smile against his lips.

Amazement brought his head up slowly, and as he looked down upon the shy brilliance lighting her dark eyes, a sense of wonderment built and spread throughout his entire body.

He'd needed her smile as much as he'd needed her loving. To have one without the other would have left him incomplete, still wanting. He'd never asked so much of a woman, and yet he needed to ask more of Blue Dalton. He wasn't going to lose her.

"Stay put," he said, rolling off of her and rising to his feet.

Without his warmth surrounding her Blue felt the chill of the morning and the embarrassment of her nakedness. Neither of which seemed to bother him. He strode across the room, the muscles in his long legs flexing with every step, the beauty of him holding her gaze. His lower body was pale compared to the golden tan of his back and arms. She blushed, thinking of how she'd touched him in the night, of all the ways he'd touched her.

He'd loved her and changed her life with the act. He'd spoken of love and changed her heart, but with the knowledge came the doubts. What did she know of the ways of men? Of the love of men? She'd given herself away in his arms, been captured by the magic he'd created with their bodies, and there was no going back to before she'd known him. She sat up and pulled the quilt around her shoulders, needing the slight protection it offered.

Behind her Walker noted the defensive action, instinctively recognizing the gesture for what it was.

"That won't work, Blue."

Her head came around, her mouth parted on a soft breath, as if he'd caught her in a lie.

"You can't hide from me. I won't let you." He walked back across the room and sank to his knees in front of her, his arms laden with the treasures of Lacey's Lode. Thick silver strands of squash blossoms hung from his wrists. Roughly carved fetishes covered his *ketoh*. Bracelets and rings filled his hands.

And he gave them all to her, one by one.

"For your first kiss," he whispered, lowering the

heaviest necklace over her head. The cool silver slid around her throat and down her chest until the crescent of silver and turquoise nestled between her breasts.

"And your second." He followed the squash-blossom necklace with a delicate strand of greenish-blue nuggets.

"For loving me last night." A slow, sexy grin teased his mouth as he layered three more necklaces on top of the other two.

"And for this morning." He leaned closer, and she felt his hands slide around her waist, and she felt the weight of a concha belt settle on her hips and dip below her waist. "Never forget this morning, Blue," he drawled, his breath followed by a lover's bite on her neck, his teeth barely grazing her skin, his tongue following the path. "This morning you were really mine."

Blue didn't know about other men, about other lovers, but she knew this man. Walker's gifts overwhelmed her, filled her with a desire to love him without boundaries, to love him with the same generosity of spirit he so easily gave.

"The letter, Walker. You saw the letter," she said softly, her cheek brushing the side of his face.

He lifted his head and met her gaze, and Blue became lost in the love she found in the amber depths shot through with green and gold. "I burned the letter. Whatever becomes of us is between you and me." He lowered his gaze to the jewelry piled between them and chose three more pieces. "For my love, Blue, I want you to wear this bracelet." His hand slid around her wrist, banding her with entwined ropes of silver and three oval stones of dark-green laced with matrix.

"And with this one"—a grin flashed across his face as he raised a ring into the firelight—"with this one I'm paying in advance for the chance you're going to give me."

Diamonds glittered in the fine circle of gold, icy hot against the roughness of his hand.

"That's not Lacey's," she said breathlessly, unable to take her eyes off the ring.

"This is the only one that ever was Lacey's. She left it to me, and I'm giving it to you, but you're going to have to ask for the rest of it." And so saying, he opened his other palm, revealing the matching wedding band. "When you're ready, you come to me and ask for it. You know the right words, don't you?"

She nodded.

"Let's hear them," he ordered softly.

"Will you marry me?" she whispered.

He took the last word from her mouth with a kiss, a slow, searching exploration of what was his, then murmured against her lips, "Be warned, Blue Dalton . . . the next time I'm going to say yes."

Eleven

"Fight, Blue. *Fight!*" Walker gripped her hand tightly, their forearms entwined, and she came half off the bed. "You can do it, sweetheart. Hold on to me."

The contraction subsided, and she sank back into the pillows. "You . . . did this . . . to me . . . on purpose," she gasped between deep breaths, holding his gaze with the glazed fire in her eyes.

"Yes, I did, and with a little luck I'll do it again," he admitted. He would have smiled if he'd had the strength, but the long day he'd spent at her side while she was in labor had left him ragged.

"Ha! Your fun is over," she moaned, and came off the bed again.

"Breathe, honey, breathe," he coached, and she panted back at him. Wild, blond hair tangled around her face and brushed her shoulders. "Breathe, breathe."

The pain relented, but she held on to him even

tighter, looking him square in the eyes. "Take me home, Walker. Take me . . . *home.*"

"I'll take you both home, but you've got to give us our baby first. You're close, so close."

"That's what you said two hours—" She started panting, her eyes growing wide. It was his fault. It was all his fault, and she'd never forgive him. Her eyes snapped shut, and her teeth grated against each other as she fought her way through another tidal wave of pain.

"You're doing great, Blue."

What did he know?

"You're going to make it. You're going to make it."

Easy for him to say!

"Hang in there, sweetheart. It's almost over."

No, it isn't! The pain keeps coming, and coming, and . . . "Take one, Walker, please. Please just take one contraction. I'm so tired. Just one," she babbled, desperate to make him understand before it was too late and the pain came again. "Just one, please."

"I'd take them all if—"

"Don't be practical. I don't need practical. I want to go home!"

She wanted to go home, with him. The words filled him with pride. He'd held on to his lady. She'd run twice during the summer, the first time she'd gotten all the way to Walden before love had brought her back to his side. The second time she'd gotten no farther than the end of the driveway. By autumn she'd started holding her ground at the front door, and when the snows of winter had come upon them, she'd been too tired and too big even to waddle that far in anger.

Yes, he'd gotten her pregnant on purpose, but she'd let him. Even as a young buck he'd never let desire overrule common sense. No other woman had ever carried his child, but no other woman had been the other half of his life. She'd come to him on a rain-swept night high in the mountains, cold, hurt, frightened, and ready to take all comers in the fight for her own survival.

And she'd come to him once more, on a cool autumn evening when the aspen leaves had danced golden and copper in the light of the setting sun, when her tummy had grown softly rounded, and she'd asked for his hand in marriage.

His mouth quirked at the memory, at his version of the facts. What she'd actually asked him for was the other half of Lacey's ring. He'd been the one exacting promises of " 'til death do us part."

"Walker, Walker, I need to push!"

"Blow, honey. Blow." He puffed his cheeks, showing her the way, and hollered over his shoulder, "Nurse!"

An hour later he cradled a miracle in the crook of his arm. His other hand lightly caressed the woman who for the seasons of a year had taught him the depths and taken him to the limits of love. Now she'd pushed him completely over the edge, where his heart floated free. He'd never felt so light. The tiny, little female nestled against his chest filled him with awe beyond measure. Every breath she took amazed him.

"Where did you get all that dark hair, sweetie? Hmmm? Has your momma been sleeping with the milkman?"

"We don't have a milkman," Blue whispered, rousing from one of the dozen or so catnaps she'd been slipping in and out of since the birth. The deep masculine voice by her bedside had been softly murmuring to their daughter every time she'd awakened. She turned to him with a tired smile. "Let me hold her."

He squeezed her hand before relinquishing his precious bundle. "Babies do smell good, all soft and warm," he said, brushing a kiss on his wife's cheek.

"She's so beautiful."

"Like her mother." He picked up her hand and held it between both of his, resting his elbows on the side of the bed. Light from the hall backlit the tousled disarray of his hair and the breadth of his shoulders beneath the pale-blue hospital gown. The square line of his jaw was dark with the stubble of his beard, giving him a rough and wild look, but nothing could diminish the gentleness in his eyes when he looked at her. "How are you feeling?"

She touched his face with her hand, smoothing his hair behind his ear. "Wonderful and happy . . . and overwhelmed with responsibility."

"You don't have to worry, Blue. I can take care of you, of you and Julie. With the sale of the North Star and Lacey's Lode, we've got enough capital behind us to take David up on his offer."

"Capital?" She chided him with a grin. "You sound like a businessman."

He returned her smile. "I may live in the middle of nowhere and make my own hours, but, honey, I've been paying taxes like the rest of the world since I was eighteen and taking city boys up into the hills. And, hell, the two years before that, I had to give my old man a cut of my guide fees for hunting on his property."

"But David wants a full-fledged guide and outfitting service. We're talking overhead and upkeep and advertising, and maybe even a lodge to house guests, not to mention partners." She slanted him a quick glance from beneath her lashes. "You're going to lose your independence."

"So are you, Blue," he said, lifting her hand to his mouth for a kiss, his gaze meeting hers. "But, to tell you the truth, I don't think we could rustle up an ounce of independence between us anymore. We've got Julie now, and I want to build something solid for the future, something solid out of the windfall of the past. We've got the land and the experience and the money to make something good for all of us, for our family."

He'd never spoken truer words. He'd found the one thing worth holding on to the night she'd entered his life with a hissed warning and a missed shot. The only woman he'd ever gone after had turned out to be the only one he needed, the one woman who by her very nature had demanded more than half a chance. Julie was the sweet culmination of their passion, but he and Blue had found more than passion to bind them. They'd shared sunrises and alpenglow, nights under the stars and days tracking the high-country meadows. They'd made love in the breathtaking vastness of the northern ranges, and the sights, sounds, and scents of the forest had never infused his senses as completely as when they were sieved through Blue's beauty and warmth, through her soft whispers and the sweetness he tasted with her every kiss. She'd been born with a will to match the wilderness she'd conquered, the one stretching up from the plains to the sky, and the one she'd laid bare in his heart.

"I love you, Annabelle Blue," he said, turning his head and tracing her palm with his lips, his voice husky with emotion.

With his child in her arms, with his strong hands holding hers she believed him. He'd left her no doubts. The one man who'd caught her had stolen her heart and given himself in its stead. She'd tried running and had been unable to leave him behind. She'd tried keeping a part of herself untouched by his love and still had found him everywhere. His life had become hers with every slowly passing day, with every hurt he'd healed until she'd become whole. He'd given her the beauty of being female, the luscious sweetness of her body when coupled with his, and he'd given her a sanctuary for the tenderness she'd so long denied. He guarded her back when she felt vulnerable. He stood by her side when she faced the rest of the world.

And then there was the magic and wonder of his love for her. He gave her the courage to love in return, and love him she did, with all her heart and soul. The emotional meshing of male and female remained a mystery to her, but a mystery she knew they'd explore together through all the changing seasons of their lives.

"Thank you, Walker. Thank you for giving me Julie," she said softly, then graced him with a sly smile and whispered even more softly, "Pretty boys make very pretty babies."

The teasing light in her eyes and the dare inherent in her words made him grin. "Yes, they do, Blue," he agreed, laughing aloud. He hadn't tamed her, not one inch of her, but he had made her his own.